MOKEE JOE

IS COMING

MOKEE JOE

IS COMING

[signature]

PETER J MURRAY

Hodder
Children's
Books

a division of Hodder Headline Limited

To my niece, Donna, for reminding me of the nightmares.

To my long-suffering wife, Kath, and to my family and friends
for putting up with my childish ways.

To Dad, who is always in my thoughts.

Copyright © 2003 Peter Murray
Illustrations © 2003 Simon Murray

First published in Great Britain in 2003
by Pen Press Publishers Ltd
This edition published by Hodder Children's Books in 2003

6 8 10 9 7 5

A Catalogue record for this book is available from the British Library

ISBN 0 340 88470 3

Typeset in Garamond by Avon DataSet Ltd,
Bidford-on-Avon, Warwickshire

Printed and bound in Great Britain by Bookmarque Ltd, Croydon, Surrey

The paper and board used in this paperback by Hodder Children's Books
are natural recyclable products made from wood grown in sustainable forests.
The manufacturing processes conform to the environmental regulations
of the country of origin.

Hodder Children's Books
a division of Hodder Headline Limited
338 Euston Road
London NW1 3BH

www.mokeejoe.com

Prologue

The two ships left within a few Earth days of each other. But such is the complexity of time and space that they landed over two hundred Earth years apart.

The escaping ship arrived first. It appeared as a fast-moving light on the edge of the marshes. It was brighter than a shooting star and its trail reached all the way to the ground. A good few of the peasants saw it, especially those living in the marshland villages. Everyone said it was a sign from the Devil and sure enough, a number of sinister events followed. For years afterwards, many of the local children reported being stalked by a ghostly figure, mostly after dark.

The chasing ship arrived during the Millennium

celebrations. People who saw it thought it was part of another firework display – though someone contacted a local newspaper and reported seeing a strange craft land in a field and then disappear. He also claimed to have seen the figures of a man and a small boy slipping away from the scene. But the witness was a well-known drunkard, and no-one believed him.

No trace of either ship was ever found.

Today the marshes have been largely drained and the only watercourse is a peaceful canal, which passes through the old borough of Danvers Green. A Norman church still survives on the outskirts of the town, which years ago would have stood on the edge of the marsh. On one of its ancient walls there hangs a plaque bearing the words:

> *Lock the door, sweet babe, shut out the night*
> *Keep the tallow candles burning bright*
> *Pray and wait for God to exercise his ploy*
> *Deliver forth the Chosen One, the Golden Boy*
> *Only he can smite the evil from this land*
> *Until that time beware the demon Mokee Man.*
>
> *(Anon. 1793)*

1

Guardian Angel

Hudson Brown lay back amongst the warm, comforting bubbles and looked towards the flickering candle perched on the edge of the bath.

'Now what do I do?' he whispered.

The voice in his head replied softly, 'Try to clear your mind of all thoughts and concentrate on the very centre of the flame.'

Hudson did exactly as he was told. He stared hard at the tiny blue triangle of light until it seemed to be the only thing that existed.

The voice of Guardian Angel continued: 'Now I'm going to chant some mystical sounds. Listen hard and concentrate on the rhythm – but keep watching the flame.'

Again, Hudson did as instructed and soon began to drift into a sleepy, dreamlike state.

'I feel really strange,' he gurgled, his mouth half-full of foam. As the soothing, rhythmic tones continued, he felt a part of himself begin to lift slowly upwards. 'This is incredible! My body feels so light, it's as if I'm floating!'

There was no sense of panic or fear, just a lovely peaceful feeling as he drifted up towards the ceiling. Soon he found himself staring at a small cobweb draped across the lampshade, right in front of his nose.

Guardian Angel's gentle, reassuring voice echoed again. 'Now I want you to will yourself to turn over and look down on your body below.'

'B-b-but I don't know how!' Hudson stammered.

'Just think it. Try to see the picture in your mind and it will happen.'

'OK – here goes . . .'

Hudson concentrated hard, trying to imagine what it would be like to see himself lying there in the bath, and the next moment he was doing exactly that. He could hardly believe his eyes.

'Wow! I can see myself. I look as if I'm asleep. This is weird! How can I be in two places at the same time?'

'You are a boy of many parts,' Guardian Angel replied, 'and you will need to draw on the strong part of yourself in the days ahead. Our mission is about to begin – our purpose in being here . . .'

But Hudson was hardly listening. He was too busy looking at his other self lying back in the soapsuds, still gazing at the candle.

Then, slowly, the words of Guardian Angel registered.

'What mission?' Hudson asked, frowning now. 'And why do I need to be strong?'

'To destroy the enemy. Tomorrow you are going to meet—'

A loud banging on the bathroom door sounded below. *'Hudson, have you fallen asleep again?'*

It was the booming voice of Mr Brown, Hudson's adoptive father. The disturbance distracted his attention and caused the voice in his head to fade, then vanish.

'Wait . . . Guardian Angel . . . don't leave me!' Hudson pleaded. 'I don't know how to get back down!'

But the voice was gone and he was alone, trapped up on the bathroom ceiling. For the first time, Hudson started to panic. Much as he loved spiders (they were his favourite creature, so purposeful), he did *not* relish the idea of spending the rest of his life up there on the ceiling with them.

A few seconds later, the bathroom door opened and Hudson saw the bald head of his father below. He watched intently as Mr Brown went over to the bath.

'It's all right!' his father muttered. 'He's dozed off again. I'll soon wake him up.'

'Oh dear, the water must have gone cold. He'll catch his death!' Hudson recognised the other voice as that of his adoptive mother, Mrs Brown.

Still trapped up on the ceiling, he watched Mr Brown go over to the sink with a flannel, run it under the cold tap and take it, dripping, over to the bath, where he began wiping the sleeping face. Hudson found to his amazement that, even up there, he could feel the cold, wet sensation. Then, before he knew what was happening, he was being drawn downwards.

'*Whoahh* . . . I'm going back! Thank God for that! *Watch out below – mind your head!'*

The next thing he knew, he was back in the bath spluttering soap bubbles and pushing away the cold flannel.

'What *are* you talking about?' Mr Brown asked sternly. 'What do you mean you're going back? And what's all this about minding heads?' He passed Hudson a towel. 'You've been dreaming again, haven't you? How do you manage to go into such a deep sleep, lad?'

'Is he all right?' Mrs Brown cried out, still waiting discreetly outside the door.

'I'm fine, Mum,' Hudson reassured her. 'I just fell asleep. I've been doing lots at school today, that's all.'

Mr Brown shook his head disapprovingly. 'Come on then. Get yourself out and let's have you dried and down those stairs, pronto. We were beginning to wonder whether you'd drowned in 'ere,' he said grumpily. 'You seem to take longer and longer over these baths, what with candles an' all, and you're always falling asleep. I've never known the likes of it!'

'Come on, Ernest, leave him alone,' called Mrs Brown. 'I'm going down to make some hot chocolate. Don't be long, Hudson.'

'I won't, Mum – just be a minute.'

'Oh yes – we know all about one of your minutes,' Mr Brown said sarcastically as he left the bathroom and made his way downstairs.

Hudson climbed out of the bath, shivering. The water had indeed gone cold but after drying himself with the big fluffy towel, he began to feel warm again. He thought about the last words Guardian Angel had said to him. Something about an enemy and meeting it tomorrow. Had the voice really said that or had he been dreaming? Perhaps the whole ceiling thing had only been a dream. It was true what his father had said – he *was* always falling asleep these days.

Peering into the mirror on the bathroom cabinet, Hudson chuckled at the sight of his hair. It was sticking out in all directions and looked like a huge mop. Picking up the towel again, he gave it a final rub and shook his head like a dog shakes its fur, so that his hair now settled into its usual style – bushing outwards, but with a parting down the middle and a second, more unusual parting, running crossways from ear to ear. He remembered the comment someone at school had made, about his head looking like a furry hot-cross bun. But it didn't worry him. Most of his friends at Danvers Green Primary thought his hairstyle looked good – especially his best friend, Molly Stevens.

Mr Brown's voice sounded from downstairs. 'Don't be all day, lad. I need to get cleaned up.'

'OK, Dad! Five minutes.'

Slipping on his stripy pyjama bottoms and looking down to where his belly button should have been, Hudson couldn't help thinking about his little 'differences', as he liked to call them. He pulled on his pyjama jacket and recalled the conversation with his mum about six months earlier.

'Mum, why don't I have a belly button like everybody else?'

'I wondered when you'd ask,' Mrs Brown had replied in an understanding voice. 'It's just one of those tiny freaks of nature, Hudson – a medical curiosity. Don't worry about it. In any case, belly buttons are no use to anyone – they only collect dust and fluff.'

But Hudson *had* worried about it and went to great trouble to keep his belly covered. He preferred other children to think he was the same as they were.

Another voice from downstairs pulled him back to the present. 'Hudson! Chocolate's ready! Don't let it go cold!'

'OK, Mum, I'm coming.'

He took down his dressing gown from the hook on the back of the bathroom door, put his watch on – Hudson always wore his watch – and went downstairs to the cosy front room of the Browns' small terraced house.

'Right, Dad, bathroom's free.'

Mr Brown put down his gardening magazine and got up from his favourite armchair by the side of the big bay window. 'At last! I can get myself cleaned up – and I won't be lighting any candles!'

Hudson chuckled to himself as his dad left the room, still muttering under his breath. He knew that Mr Brown cared for him dearly and only grumbled to hide his concern.

Mrs Brown ushered Hudson over to the coffee table, where there was a tray containing a huge steaming mug and a plate of biscuits. 'Here, get this while it's hot,' she said, going over to the polished oak sideboard and taking out her knitting bag.

'Thanks, Mum.' Hudson held his mug in both hands and sipped the hot, sweet chocolate. He looked thoughtful. After a few minutes, he glanced up to see his mother sitting by his side, clicking her knitting needles furiously and looking into his hazel eyes with a slightly worried expression. It had always fascinated him how quickly her fingers worked with the needles, and how she never needed to look down at what she was doing.

'Are you OK, Mum?'

'I'm fine,' she replied in her usual gentle way. 'The question is – are *you*? You seem to be having one of your "thinking periods".'

Hudson nodded and continued to sip his drink. His mother always knew when something was bothering him. He sometimes wondered if she could read his mind – like Guardian Angel.

'What is it, Hudson? Are you worrying about that belly button again?'

Hudson shook his head. 'No, it's just that I feel a bit funny about tomorrow – I don't know why. My stomach's churning a bit.'

He could see the concern in Mrs Brown's eyes. The needles clicked on.

'Well, I can't think why either.' She was trying to make him feel better. 'Anyway, it's Saturday tomorrow – no school, so that can't be bad. Just keep yourself out of trouble.' She stopped her knitting for a second and patted his shoulder. 'And you know, don't you, that we're always here for you if you need us.'

Hudson nodded. Mr and Mrs Brown were so kind to him. He considered himself very lucky to have them, though he often wondered about his real parents. He still had no idea where he really came from – there was just a great big blank in his mind as far as that was concerned, which sometimes made him feel very lonely. Maybe one day someone would be able to give him a few answers.

He finished his chocolate, put his cup on the table and fiddled with his watch. When he had thoroughly checked and adjusted all the time settings, he reached over and picked up Pugwash. The jet-black cat purred with contentment as he stroked its fur and settled back to watch TV.

Half an hour later, Mrs Brown put down her knitting. 'I think it's about time you were off to bed now, Hudson,' she said, picking up the tray and heading for the kitchen. 'No doubt Molly will be around early.'

Hudson cheered up at the thought of Molly. She had been his best friend since they'd first met at football practice, and they spent practically all their time together. Molly was strong-willed and as tough as any boy he knew – probably a lot tougher than most. Hudson liked her determination, which matched his own. In fact, at this very moment, the thought of it was strangely reassuring. And Molly seemed to think a lot of him too. Of course she would never say so, there was no chance of that, but he knew it all the same.

No doubt she would want to go to the Castle tomorrow, as they usually did. Hudson might argue with her a bit, just so she didn't get her way too easily, but he would agree in the end because the Castle was their favourite local spot.

As he walked upstairs, carrying Pugwash, a shiver suddenly hurried down his spine and the nervous feeling fluttered in his stomach again. Like butterflies trying to get out.

'I wish I knew what Guardian Angel had tried to warn me about before we were cut off,' he said, talking to Pugwash. He went on mumbling to himself, trying to remember their conversation, as the cat gazed up at him with a wide-eyed, puzzled expression. 'Something about a mission and meeting an enemy.'

But Pugwash really wasn't that interested in missions or enemies, and he wriggled out of Hudson's arms. He leapt down the stairs and Hudson heard the back door open and close as Mrs Brown let him outside.

Before getting into bed that night, Hudson looked out of his bedroom window. The night sky looked beautiful, crisp and clear, and he found his eyes drawn to a group of stars. One seemed to twinkle more brightly than the rest and he couldn't stop staring at it. For some reason this distant, shimmering light made him feel very lonely. He suddenly felt sad and wanted someone to hug him.

The spell was broken by a noise from below and he looked down. He thought he saw a shadow creeping about in the alleyway beneath his window. Suddenly he got goosebumps and the hairs on the back of his neck stood on end.

Surely it was Pugwash, wasn't it? No – it was too big to be a cat. Hudson always kept a torch on his desk and he reached over for it. He switched it on and aimed it downwards, using it as a miniature searchlight. But there was nothing to see. Perhaps it had been his imagination playing tricks. He was certainly feeling jumpy enough.

Quickly drawing the curtains, he climbed into bed and pulled the duvet over his face. He tried to concentrate his thoughts on his special friend – Guardian Angel. Focusing his mind, as he had done with the candle, he tried to contact him again, but nothing happened.

Finally, just as he was sinking into sleep, a piercing shriek shattered the silence of his bedroom as something heavy landed on the bed.'

2

King of the castle

'But how did he get through if you'd closed the window?'
Molly asked, cuddling Pugwash.

Hudson looked into Molly's big, brown eyes. She was
a confident, pretty ten-year-old, and it fascinated him the
way she wore her jet-black hair in a single bunch that
sprouted out of the top of her head like pineapple
leaves. He thought it looked fantastic.

'That's just it,' Hudson answered. 'I closed the curtains
but I forgot to close the window. It was still wide enough
for Pugwash to come flying through. Something out
there gave him a real fright.'

'It must have given *you* a real fright when he landed
on your bed!' Molly laughed, cuddling the cat close to
her face. 'Who's a naughty boy then?'

The cat purred loudly.

'It's not funny, Molly. And there's something else bothering me at the moment. But I don't know whether to tell you about it – you'll probably just start laughing again!'

Molly put the cat down and Hudson watched her brush the hairs off her jeans. He really liked those jeans – covered in silver stars from her feet up to her knees. They made her look trendy, yet different from all the other girls.

'No I won't, I promise,' she said, standing up and pacing around restlessly. 'Look, I'm fed up hanging round here!' Hudson knew what was coming next. 'Let's go to the Castle and you can tell me about it on the way.'

'OK, I'll just ask Mum if she needs anything – won't be a minute.'

He found Mrs Brown in the kitchen, relaxing with a cup of coffee and a magazine. 'Mum, do you need us to go to the Castle?'

'Well, I wouldn't mind actually. But what about that funny feeling of yours? Perhaps you and Molly should stay round here today – just to be on the safe side.'

'No, it'll be fine, Mum. I don't know what was wrong with me yesterday.' He tucked his shirt into his jeans and began fiddling with his watch.

She smiled at him and Hudson thought at first that it was her 'motherly' smile, loving and slightly indulgent. But then he realised it was more of an accepting smile, as if she sensed her son was not quite like other children, and must sometimes be allowed to get on with things in his own way.

Hudson was pleased – he was definitely getting better at reading people's thoughts.

'Go on then,' she said. 'Go and get a piece of paper and a pencil while I have a think what we need.'

Hudson went to fetch them and came back a few minutes later with Molly beside him. 'OK, Mum, ready.'

Molly looked over his shoulder as he prepared to write.

'Half a dozen eggs,' Mrs Brown began, 'and a large . . . no, a small bottle of cooking oil. A jar of—'

'Not too fast, Mum!'

'Sorry!' She paused, sipped her coffee and began again, this time more slowly, 'Half a dozen eggs. A small bottle of cooking oil. And get a jar of that jam your dad likes, you know which one. Oh, and a bag of self-raising flour as well. That'll do for now, it's plenty for you to carry.' She stood up. 'I'll just get my purse.'

Hudson still hadn't finished writing. Molly tugged at the sleeve of his red and black tartan shirt. 'Hudson! Your mum only said four things but you've written five. What's that last bit?'

Hudson picked up the list and started reading it back. There was a trace of a tremor in his voice. 'Half a dozen eggs, a small cooking oil, Dad's jam, self-raising flour, *Mokee Joe is coming*!'

'Why have you written that? Who's Mokee Joe?' Molly asked, frowning at Hudson.

Hudson scratched his ear with his pencil and looked puzzled. 'I haven't a clue.'

Just then, Mrs Brown returned with her purse. 'Hudson, is everything all right?' She had seen the strange look on his face and had also noticed that he was playing with his watch again.

'Fine, Mum, no problem. Ready, Molly?'

Molly replied with her usual energy and enthusiasm. 'He's just scared I'm going to beat him in a race, Mrs Brown – that's all.' She adjusted her hairband, tilting her head down as she looked across at him, which made her eyes look even bigger. 'Right, I'm ready, Hudson. I'll give you five seconds' start and I'll still beat you to the trolley park. I'll bring the money – you go! *One, two, three . . .*'

Hudson was glad of Molly's little ruse; he didn't want to worry his mum any more. He tore off down Tennyson Road and, as he looked back, he could see Molly hurtling through the garden gate, hot on his tail.

For the moment, all strange thoughts were forgotten. Hudson was just a ten-year-old boy being challenged by a ten-year-old girl. What mattered now was getting to the supermarket before her, and Molly was a tough competitor. If she beat him, he'd never hear the end of it.

Five minutes later, as Molly tried desperately to close the last few yards on him, Hudson almost fell into the trolley park of the Castle Supermarket.

'Made it!' he panted.

'Only just!' Molly gasped. 'I gave you too big a start.'

The two friends sat on a wall surrounding the long lines of supermarket trolleys.

'So what's all this about then?' Molly asked, still breathing heavily. 'Is it something to do with that weird name you wrote on the shopping list – what was it – Monkey Joe?'

'No – *Mokee* Joe,' Hudson replied. 'Come on, let's go over to the swings and I'll tell you about it – only you've got to promise to keep it to yourself.'

Molly folded her arms, side-stepped and charged with her shoulder into Hudson's side, catching him unawares so that he stumbled over. 'Come on – I bet I can go higher than you on the swings!' she teased.

The two friends set off for the small adventure playground by the side of the car park. They sat side by side on the swings, and as Molly detected Hudson's more serious mood, she briefly forgot their friendly rivalry.

Hudson carried on from where he'd left off. 'I've been having some bad feelings,' he said, frowning. 'I know it sounds stupid, but I'm beginning to think it's got something to do with this place.' He glanced back over his shoulder towards the supermarket.

Molly started to swing a little higher. 'Don't be so daft,' she grinned at him. 'What could go wrong in a supermarket?'

'Can you keep another secret?' Hudson asked, now swinging harder himself, trying to catch her up.

'You know I can – if you really want me to.' Molly trailed her feet on the ground and stopped swinging.

Hudson did the same. He leaned across and whispered. 'Well, I know it sounds crazy, but there's this voice that sometimes warns me about things and last night—'

Molly interrupted. There was now a flicker of genuine interest in her eyes. 'Hang on! What do you mean by "voice"? Can anyone hear it?'

'No – only me,' he replied. 'I call it Guardian Angel.'

Molly screwed her nose up. 'Why Guardian Angel?'

'Well, I heard Mum say that everyone has a Guardian Angel to watch over them and so I reckon this voice in my head must be mine.'

Molly bent down to tie one of the laces on her trainers.

'But that's only a saying, Hudson. Guardian Angels aren't real, you must know *that*.'

'This one is,' Hudson replied in a challenging tone. 'When I concentrate really hard it speaks to me. And I'm getting better – I can hear it more and more.'

'And what sort of things does it say?' Molly asked, fixing her eyes on Hudson's.

Hudson was really earnest now. 'That's what I'm trying to tell you! Last night it warned me that I'm going to meet an enemy – *today*!'

'Mokee Joe, I suppose,' Molly suggested flippantly, starting to swing again. 'Well, if you ask me, you've been playing too many computer games and your imagination's gone ballistic.'

Hudson started fiddling with his watch again. 'Well, all the same, I'm not sure we should go in there. Perhaps we should get Mum's shopping from the corner shop on the way home.'

Molly stopped swinging, and Hudson could see a faint look of exasperation on her face. She unzipped a pocket in front of her hoody and took out a small, heart-shaped purse, from which she took a neatly-folded five-pound note.

'Look – it's only going to take a few minutes,' she said impatiently. 'You get the cooking oil and the jam, and I'll get the eggs and flour. We'll meet back at the check-out in five minutes. Just forget about angels and voices for now, OK?'

Hudson laughed in spite of himself. Normally they were equally confident, neither one more of a leader than the other. But today, for some reason, he felt comforted by Molly's assertiveness.

They jumped off the swings and headed for the entrance of the supermarket. As they passed through the huge automatic doors, Hudson stood in front of the long row of check-outs and scanned around. Everything looked normal. He threaded his hands together and bent his fingers back so that the joints cracked loudly.

'Hudson, don't do that, *pu-l-ease*!' Molly pleaded. 'You know I can't stand it!'

But Hudson never even heard her. He was too busy looking around. He tried to tell himself that if danger really lurked inside, loads of people would be around to help – and Guardian Angel would most likely be on stand-by.

'OK, see you back here in five minutes. And *stop looking like such a scaredy cat*!' Molly grinned at him. She passed through the shiny metal turnstile and disappeared up one of the aisles.

If Molly enjoyed going to the Castle because of the playground, Hudson liked to go there for another reason. Whenever they went into the supermarket, he always imagined that he was the manager. He loved the idea of being in charge. He knew that his fantasy was probably a bit silly, and perhaps this was why it was a secret he shared with no-one – not even Molly.

And now Hudson needed his game more than ever – something to take his mind off that uneasy feeling he had.

As Molly set off to collect the flour and eggs, Manager Hudson strode down the aisles checking that everything was in order. And everything *was* in order – completely normal.

He pushed all thoughts of enemies, missions and

Mokee Joe out of his mind – it was just his imagination, as Molly had said. She was right: what *could* possibly go wrong in a place like this?

He began to relax and went back to his game, imagining that the supermarket staff were under *his* command. As he walked past the cold meat counter he gave a regal wave to a woman who was carving some ham from a large joint.

'Carry on,' he said quietly as he walked by. She heard him and gave him a strange look.

A little further on, another woman in a smart suit was holding a plate of cheese, offering samples for people to taste. Hudson took one of the little sticks and pulled the strong-smelling Cheddar off with his teeth. It tasted delicious.

'This is excellent,' he said in his most formal voice. 'Please tell the supplier that I am more than pleased.'

The woman laughed and offered him another piece.

Continuing his walkabout and heading up an aisle towards where the cooking oil was stacked, Hudson saw that one of his staff was building a huge pyramid of baked bean cans. 'Well done, young man,' Hudson said with authority. 'You've almost reached the top. Carry on.'

The man muttered something but didn't look round. He was too busy concentrating.

Further up the aisle, Hudson passed a customer searching through some packets on a shelf. Her baby was sitting in her shopping trolley, crying impatiently. He considered offering her some assistance.

But then a figure at the very end of the aisle caught his attention, and held it. His heart began to beat faster.

It was stooping over a frozen food compartment with

its back turned towards him. Even leaning forward, it seemed inhumanly tall and was wearing a long scruffy raincoat, tied at the waist with a piece of string. It looked like a skeleton in outdoor clothes.

Whoahh . . . I don't like the look of him, thought Hudson, beginning to feel very fidgety. He looked around anxiously, wondering where Molly was. She was nowhere in sight.

Suddenly, all the fears he had pushed out of his mind came creeping back. He knew instinctively that the figure in front of him had something to do with Guardian Angel's warning . . . and now something awful was about to happen.

3

The Great Escape

As Hudson continued to stare at the stooping form, he noticed a faint blue glow beginning to shimmer around it.

Enemy . . . Mission . . . he kept thinking. *This is what Guardian Angel was warning me about. I just know it is.*

He took in its appearance more fully now. Black hair fell in greasy strands from a wide-brimmed hat and hung limply over the upturned collar of the filthy grey coat. Two shabby trouser legs stuck out from the bottom of the coat into a pair of massive, grubby boots. There was also an unpleasant burning smell that seemed to be emanating from the figure.

Wow, he looks weird just from the back, Hudson muttered to himself. He decided he wouldn't mind at all if he never got to see it from the front.

A tap on his shoulder made him jump round, and there was Molly, clutching a carton of eggs.

'Hudson! Are you getting the shopping, or what?' she said, then: 'What's wrong, what are you staring at?'

'Sshh . . . Look . . . there . . . in front – it's the thing Guardian Angel's been warning me about!'

Molly followed his gaze, then giggled. 'What are you on about?'

He looked back at the freezer. *There was no-one there!*

Hudson was baffled. 'Molly, honest . . .'

'Oh, Hudson,' Molly scolded him playfully, 'you know you can't scare me that easy! Come on, let's get the rest of the stuff and then we can get out of this *cree-ee-py* place,' she teased.

'This isn't a joke, Molly, I mean it, there really was . . .' His voice trailed off as he looked at the amused sparkle in her big eyes. He didn't want to look a dork – or, worse, a coward – in front of Molly. 'Oh, all right, come on – the jam and the flour are over there.'

He picked up a small bottle of oil from a nearby shelf, then they found the apple and blackberry jam his father liked so much.

But then, as Hudson turned the next corner to get the flour, with Molly following close behind, he suddenly saw, to his horror, a wide-brimmed black hat hovering above the shelves in the next aisle. There was no doubt it was the same hat he'd just seen – who else could possibly be that tall? – and the sight of it, haloed by that crackling blue glow, made him feel sick. He stopped dead in his tracks and Molly walked straight into the back of him.

'Hudson! You nearly made me drop the eggs! Now what's up?'

But it was no use. As Hudson pointed, the hat disappeared, as if the wearer had suddenly ducked down.

'I just saw . . . Oh, what's the point! I know you'll never believe me. But I'm telling you, we really do have to get out of here.'

Hudson turned and looked at his friend, waiting for a smart retort. But Molly was just standing there with her mouth wide open, her clear brown eyes wide with fright.

'God, Hudson, I think you're right! There's something weird going on – I don't like it!'

As he turned back, following Molly's gaze, Hudson saw that the strange blue glow had reappeared, and was crackling loudly above a stack of tinned tunafish, causing sparks to fly off the metal.

Hudson felt hollow inside as he watched the blue light rise higher into the air, and the now familiar hat appear beneath it. And then, as he and Molly stood frozen to the spot, the hat seemed to float away towards the far end of the aisle . . . *and began to turn the corner towards them!*

'Oh my God, what is it?' was all Molly could say.

Suddenly, the sinister silhouette that Hudson had seen earlier appeared at the end of the aisle. Though still surrounded by a blue glow, it looked blurred and shadowy, its face hidden under the hat and shielded by the upturned collar of the dirty grey coat. Now, seeing it standing straight, Hudson's blood ran cold as he estimated that it was at least seven feet tall!

Molly grabbed his arm. 'Hudson, I think it's staring at us!'

All thoughts of being the supermarket manager were forgotten; Hudson was just a ten-year-old boy out shopping for his mum – and he didn't want to be here any more.

'Molly, tell me this is a nightmare and I'm going to wake up in a minute.'

'I wish I could, but I've got a horrible feeling it might be real,' Molly whispered loudly, now tugging urgently at his arm.

He looked back again at the staring figure. It was still there, yet nobody else seemed to be taking any notice of it. *Can't they see it?* wondered Hudson. *And if not, how can it be real?*

And then, to his horror, it started taking big strides towards them.

'HUDSON! IT'S COMING TO GET US! *RUN!*'

As the thing drew closer, it reached out its arms and the frayed coat sleeves slipped back to reveal bony, pincer-like hands. Its long fingers crackled, sending out streaks of lethal blue electricity. Several cereal packets shuddered and fell from their shelf, to be crushed under the creature's passing boots.

Though terrified, Hudson knew he must somehow focus his mind. He did, and just for a second he heard the familiar voice in his head: *'This is your enemy – the Mokee Man. You must run to escape. Disturb the tower!'*

As the menacing figure moved ever closer, its face still in shadow, Hudson remained rooted to the spot. He felt the tingling of electricity as his hair stood on end even more than usual.

Finally he reacted. 'OK! LET'S LEG IT!' he yelled.

He grabbed Molly's hand and they started sprinting back down the aisle. But the gaunt figure was almost upon them and Hudson knew he had to act fast.

Disturb the tower. 'I've got to disturb the tower!' he shouted as they ran.

'*What?*' Molly yelled.

They ran, weaving in and out of the aisles, until suddenly Hudson saw someone crouching in front of them. It was the man who had been building the baked bean can pyramid, and he was just about to put the last tin on top.

Hudson pulled Molly with him and deliberately forced a collision. An explosive clatter followed as exactly one-hundred-and-seventy-four cans of baked beans came crashing down onto the floor.

'*I DID IT!*' Hudson shouted to no-one in particular. 'I disturbed the tower!'

The two friends stopped and looked back.

There was utter chaos as the store assistant and the woman with the baby went sprawling, floundering helplessly on a sea of baked bean tins. They were soon joined by more customers, who skidded and fell as they passed. The baby in the trolley stopped crying and gurgled with delight.

The pursuing figure had vanished.

Molly grabbed Hudson's arm. 'Quick, Hudson, let's get out of here. It's probably still after us!'

Hudson knew she was right. The creature would surely not give up so easily.

Suddenly Molly gasped in his ear. '*It's back– right behind us!*'

The gangly figure was striding towards them now, but Hudson had already spotted the contents of a nearby shelf. Bags of flour: plain flour, self-raising flour, all types of flour.

'Quick – a missile!'

'*What?*' Molly cried.

'Mum's flour – I need it now!'

Picking up the nearest bag, he turned and threw it with all his might.

It was an excellent shot. Hudson and Molly watched open-mouthed as the heavy bag of self-raising flour struck their pursuer full in the face, bursting as it did so with remarkable effect. There was a blinding blue flash and the air filled with clouds of white dust.

'BRILLIANT!' Molly yelled.

'Yes and look, he's down!' Hudson added, with an air of triumph.

They both watched in fascination as the creature sank onto the floor in front of them – but almost willingly. It seemed, in fact, to be *basking* in the flour that cascaded down over its head!

Now Molly was clinging to Hudson's arm and pointing. 'Look!'

Hudson stared. The flour was beginning to disappear. It was as though the creature was absorbing the white powder through its mouth, its skin, even through its shabby clothes. Then it turned onto all fours and began crawling around, sucking up every last particle, like a revolting, living vacuum cleaner.

Now it rose menacingly to its feet again, this time glowing bright purple and looking even taller than before. It was as if the flour had recharged it – given it more energy. And as the creature stood there, shoppers began to gather round and stare, their hands covering their mouths in horror.

The chase wasn't over.

In panic, Hudson cried, '*Oh, God*, Molly! Look! That flour seems to have given it more power!'

Molly didn't have time to agree. The thing was coming at them again.

This time it was Molly's turn to act. Still clutching the egg carton, she launched her own attack. 'OK, Mr Mokee . . . whatever your name is,' she seethed through gritted teeth. 'How d'you like your eggs – scrambled?'

As the monster ran at them again, the first egg whistled close to its head and missed; but the remainder all found their target. Five large, fresh eggs splattered straight into its powdery face, making it a gooey mess of runny eggs and flour. Temporarily blinded, the creature stopped dead in its tracks and tried to clear its vision.

'OK!' Molly yelled. 'It's time we were out of here and this time, Hudson . . . *I won't be giving you a start!*'

Seconds later, the two friends had reached the exit and Hudson took a last look over his shoulder at the chaotic scene.

A uniformed security man had arrived and was shouting frantically into a mobile. The store assistant was trying to pick up his baked bean cans and at the same time calm the baby's mother, who was screaming hysterically and demanding to see the manager. A crowd of shocked onlookers wittered in high-pitched tones as a tall, electric-blue figure ran across to the exit and crashed its way out onto the street. Only the baby in the trolley chortled with glee, enjoying all the entertainment.

At the exit, Hudson and Molly just ran and ran. They never even realised that they'd come away without a single item of Mrs Brown's shopping.

* * *

A short while later, two breathless children arrived on the doorstep of number 13, Tennyson Road. As Hudson barged through the front door, he looked up and saw his mum standing there with her mouth wide open.

'What on Earth's happened? You two look like you've just seen a ghost!'

Hudson looked helplessly at Molly. No words would come into his head.

'Sorry about that, Mrs Brown,' Molly said with a wry smile. 'It's my fault. I challenged Hudson to another race on the way back and he just lost by about ten metres.'

Hudson looked sheepish. Leaving Molly in the sitting room, he went through to the kitchen and poured them each a large glass of water.

'Well, where's the shopping?' Mrs Brown asked, following him into the kitchen.

Hudson took a sip from his glass. 'Sorry, Mum. I sort of dropped it on the way.'

'You *dropped* it – *all* of it?' Mrs Brown looked at him suspiciously. 'Hudson, is there something you're not telling me?'

'No, it's nothing, Mum.' He sipped from his glass again. 'It's just that when Molly's around, we get carried away with challenges and everything. You know.' And he shrugged.

Mrs Brown tutted and reminded him that their evening meal would suffer as a result of the shopping being lost. But she didn't go on about it for too long, and Hudson sensed that, though she was puzzled, she was in some way sympathetic.

He rejoined Molly, looking at her shocked face. 'Well,

now do you believe me about Guardian Angel and Mokee Joe?' he whispered.

Molly gawped at him and just nodded.

And then, as she was drinking her water, she suddenly started to splutter and choke. She pointed out of the window; Hudson turned and followed her finger. There, on the other side of the road, leaning carelessly against a lamppost, was the tall, emaciated outline of his enemy. The face was still in shadow, but the hairs on the back of Hudson's neck stood on end as he realised, without a doubt, that it was *staring straight at him.*

4

One, two, three, four, five..............

The following morning Hudson and Molly were together in their favourite meeting place – the garden shed at the bottom of the Browns' garden. They referred to it as Candleshed and regarded it as their most private space.

Hudson was deep in thought as Molly lit the red candle and placed it in the middle of the rough wooden table. He looked at his watch. It was only 10.30am, but the day was dark and overcast, and everything seemed shrouded in gloom. The only sound was his father digging somewhere up the garden.

'OK, let's get down to business,' Hudson said in a sombre tone.

Molly blew out the match, sat down opposite Hudson

and looked at him, her chin propped in her hands.

'So that creep in the supermarket – that was Mokee Joe then?' Molly began.

'Yes, I'm sure it was. I mean, was that scary or what? And then after all that – the way he followed us home and just stood there across the road . . .'

Molly put her little finger in her mouth and chewed at the nail. 'I thought he would never go. He must have hung around for at least an hour. It's funny how he vanished just as you were thinking of getting your mum to phone the police.'

'I know.'

'It was as if he could read your mind.'

'I know,' Hudson repeated, beginning to adjust his watch.

'Hudson, what's all this about? Why is this thing after you?'

Hudson scratched his head. He glanced over Molly's shoulder towards the cracked mirror hanging on the wall of the shed.

'I've no idea. But I've got a feeling I'm going to find out soon. I suppose I always knew I was different and that one day something strange like this would happen.'

'What do you mean – "different"?'

Hudson stared into the mirror. His hair was sticking out in all directions. 'Well – where do I start?' He began to fidget in his chair. 'First, how many people do you know called Hudson?'

Molly shrugged. 'None – but that's no big deal. It's a cool name.'

'And then I don't remember anything of what happened before I came to Mum and Dad's.'

'Yes, but loads of people can't remember being babies,' Molly reminded him, adjusting her hairband.

'But I can't remember anything before I was *seven*! And I don't even know who my real parents are or where I come from.'

Hudson stood up and began to pace around the shed.

'OK, I see what you mean,' Molly replied, following him round with her eyes.

'And then there's the voice in my head – Guardian Angel.'

'But that's good, isn't it, Hudson – having someone to watch over you? Your mum said so, remember?'

Hudson sat down again, threaded his hands together and bent his fingers back so that his knuckles cracked loudly. Molly gritted her teeth but didn't ask him to stop.

'Well, it would be if I wasn't being threatened by this nightmare. But it's like I really *need* a Guardian Angel now.'

Molly took a tube of mints from the top pocket of her faded denim jacket and offered them across the table. Hudson accepted one and popped it in his mouth.

'All this seems so unreal,' he said. 'Can you believe it's happening? It's like something out of a science fiction video!'

Molly sucked hard on her mint and played with it between her lips. 'I know. When I woke up this morning I had to convince myself it hadn't all just been a bad dream.' She paused. 'You know what, I think I'm going to up my judo sessions to three times a week.'

Good old Molly, Hudson thought. *If anyone can sort that creep out, it's her*. She was gutsy enough to look after the both of them, though as a team they'd be invincible.

'D'you think we should tell the oldies what happened?' she continued.

'No – not yet. I mean, the supermarket manager will probably have reported everything to the police anyway, but let's keep this to ourselves for as long as we can.'

Molly began to crunch her mint. She was looking at Hudson quite intently, with a half-smile, and for no apparent reason, he felt himself begin to blush.

He hastily averted his eyes, only to find himself confronted by his reflection in the cracked mirror. It had suddenly grown darker, and he was intrigued by how piercing his eyes looked.

Molly grinned at him. 'We all know you're gorgeous, Hudson – you can stop admiring yourself!'

Just then, the light in the shed began to dim and the air grew heavy, charged with an eerie silence. Hudson's eyes widened as the image in the glass began to distort and change.

'Molly!' he breathed.

'Hudson – what's *wrong*? You look really *weird*!'

'It's the mirror!'

As Hudson continued to stare, a face different from his own slowly materialised, until a strange, bald-headed man gazed back at him. The face was plump and quite old, but it was the eyes that alarmed him most.

'What *is* it?' Molly asked frantically. 'Hudson – what can you see?' She swivelled round in her chair so that she too was facing the mirror.

'A face. The eyes are just white! No pupils or anything. They're staring right into mine!'

Molly peered into the dusty glass. She could only see her own large brown eyes reflected back. 'Where? I can't see anything.'

Hudson was now on his feet, leaning forward, straining to see more. 'It's fading – it's . . . it's gone. But it was there, I saw it!'

Molly reached over, grabbed his wrist and pulled him back into a sitting position. 'Hudson, it's OK.'

Hudson relaxed a bit. 'Yes, it's OK,' he repeated. Then, almost calmly, he said, 'Molly, I think I've just seen the face of Guardian Angel. Don't ask me how I know – I just do!'

At that moment, the shed door began to creak open. As a large shape loomed outside the window, Molly grasped Hudson's wrist tighter. The two friends locked eyes and mouthed the words '*Mokee Joe*'.

The door burst open.

'Refreshments!'

A smiling Mrs Brown stood outside the door, holding a tray containing two mugs of hot chocolate and a plate of biscuits.

'Hudson, nip up to the house, will you?' she said as she put the tray down. 'Ashley's on the phone and he's desperate to talk to you. He said it's urgent.'

Hudson sprinted up the garden and went indoors. He sensed that somehow this phone call was connected with everything that had happened.

Panting a bit, he picked up the receiver. 'Hello? Ash?'

A familiar voice crackled back down the phone. 'Hi, Hudson. Are you coming up this afternoon? I'm fishing at the usual spot, near the iron bridge.'

'Sounds good to me – I'll be there later with Molly,'

Hudson replied, still trying to catch his breath. 'Is everything OK?'

'Funny you should say that,' Ash replied. 'Only this crazy guy turned up earlier, on the towpath. Luckily he didn't come too close, but there was definitely something weird about him.'

Hudson's brain started working furiously. 'What did he look like?'

'Well, all I could see was that he looked scruffy, and sort of freakish – really tall.'

Hudson tried hard to keep his voice calm. He didn't want to panic his friend. 'Look, Ash – I think you'd better—'

Ash interrupted, his voice growing fainter. 'Hey . . . we're beginning to break up. I wanted to tell you about this strange text message I got just after—'

But Hudson heard no more. The signal on Ash's mobile had gone.

He put down the phone and headed back towards Candleshed. 'I don't like it,' he kept muttering to himself. He would tell Molly, and they'd go straight up the canal that afternoon.

Hudson did not enjoy his Sunday lunch. The phone call from Ash had unsettled him. He barely touched his Yorkshire pudding or his mum's homemade apple and blackberry crumble, which caused plenty of grumbling from Mr Brown and raised eyebrows from his wife.

Hudson insisted his loss of appetite was due to a matter of urgent business he needed to attend to, but his father was having none of it.

'Urgent business at your age!' Mr Brown spluttered,

spitting half the contents of his mouth all over the table. 'I've never heard the likes of it! In my day—'

But Mrs Brown cut her husband short as usual and allowed Hudson to leave the table, though not before he had promised to be home early. She reminded him it was school tomorrow and he wasn't the best at getting up in the morning.

What with all that was happening, Hudson felt heartened by the mention of school. School was *real* and right now he needed all the reality he could get.

By 2.15pm, Molly was almost running up the towpath of the Danvers and Dearne Canal to keep up with Hudson's determined stride.

'D'you really think Ash is in trouble?' she asked breathlessly.

Hudson looked up at the black clouds rolling overhead. 'Well, if my instincts are right, I think he could be.' He pulled the hood of his bright red waterproof over his head and drew the tie cord under his chin. Molly, wearing a silver waterproofed hoody, did the same.

Big raindrops began to dimple the surface of the canal. Molly caught hold of Hudson's arm, slowing him down. 'But what makes you feel that? Has GA been in contact again?'

Hudson picked up on the abbreviation immediately. It was always like that with him and Molly – their minds seemed to work in the same way. 'No. It's just too much of a coincidence, that's all. First the message on the shopping list and then that thing in the supermarket. Now Ash sees a creepy figure on the towpath and says he got a strange message on his mobile.'

'Mmm, you're probably right. Come on, let's speed up.'

Hudson started taking even bigger strides and Molly broke into a gentle jog to keep pace. Ten minutes later, they reached the old brickworks. The iron bridge was about five minutes further on.

As they approached the derelict factory on the corner of Kiln Street, a huge billboard loomed in front of them. Hudson glanced up at it and stopped dead. It was advertising a sweet called a Space Bar, and there was a picture of a spacecraft descending from a starlit sky into a field of cows. Underneath was written: '*Space Bars are made the milkiest way.*'

Molly tugged at his arm. 'Hudson, what's up now?'

He stared up at the picture, his eyes drawn towards the giant curved windscreen of the spaceship.

'Hudson, come *on*! Ash'll be wondering where we are!'

But Hudson didn't answer. He was captivated by the two alien figures in the front of the ship. He couldn't explain why, but right at that moment those two figures seemed very significant.

And then the heavens opened. It began to pour with rain and Hudson snapped out of his trance. 'Sorry, just dreaming. Quick, let's run. Hope Ash has got his big fishing umbrella with him.'

Thunder rumbled somewhere overhead and the raindrops stretched into silver rods, spearing the ground and bouncing off the inky surface of the canal. Hudson and Molly peered through the watery curtain ahead, and could just make out Ash's large green fishing umbrella and the iron bridge in the distance.

Moments later, he and Molly were huddled under the dripping canvas by Ash's side.

'Hey, am I glad to see you two!' Ash grinned nervously, showing a wide row of white teeth. He put his fishing rod on the rests, sat down and ran his hand through his hair from front to back. This was a habit of Ash's which (whether he knew it or not) made him look a bit like Hudson – though minus the special parting.

'So come on, what exactly's been happening?' Hudson asked impatiently.

Molly untied her hood and fluffed up the bunch on top of her head. 'Yes, come on, tell us.'

'Well, the fishing was quite good this morning. I was catching some good perch and a few nice roach when this crazy guy showed up – you know, the one I told you about.'

'Tell me again what he looked like,' Hudson insisted.

The thunder rumbled again, but now sounded closer.

'Like a tramp. Old clothes, really dirty – you know what I mean?'

Hudson looked at Molly.

'And why "crazy"?' Molly urged. 'What was he doing that was so crazy?'

Ash began to fidget nervously on his fishing box. 'Well, I don't know . . . I mean, I could see he was throwing stones at some ducks and then he'd just stop and stand there, staring down the towpath at me.'

'And then what?'

Ash stood up, reached inside his fishing box and took out his mobile. 'Well, then he disappeared, but just after that I got this really weird text message. Here – look.' And he passed the phone to Hudson.

A big raindrop dripped onto the mobile from Hudson's spiky hair and trickled across the glass, temporarily blurring the words. Hudson read the familiar message, a slight tremor in his voice:

'*Mokee Joe is coming!*'

5

Water, Water, Everywhere

Hudson passed Ash's mobile to Molly and watched her shocked expression.

'Hey, what's all this about? You two look really worried,' said Ash, who was looking more worried than anyone.

'Ash, you really don't want to know,' Molly answered.

The rain stopped and the sun tried to make an appearance. Hudson stepped outside Ash's brolly and looked up towards the iron bridge. Angry black clouds loomed in the distance, threatening more rain to come.

But most threatening of all was the tall, wasted figure poised on the bridge.

Molly saw immediately. 'It's him, isn't it?'

Even from that distance, the black hat, stringy hair and

shabby coat with upturned collar were clearly visible. Hudson had no doubt who it was that was staring at them. He looked back at Molly and saw his own worst fears reflected in her expression.

Ash looked too and shouted, *'That's him! That's the guy!'*

Hudson turned to Ash and said very calmly, 'Look, we have to get out of here. How long will it take you to pack up your fishing tackle?'

Ash's eyes opened wide. 'At . . . at least ten minutes.'

A flock of seagulls, inland for the winter, screeched high above the iron bridge. The menacing figure was now edging its way down the steps of the rusty structure. Once at the bottom, it planted its massive feet on the towpath. The seagulls wheeled above its head as if warding it off, yet afraid to get too close.

Molly gasped. 'HUDSON! HE'S COMING!'

Ash, who was smaller than the other two, cowered behind them and peered round their backs as the creature started advancing slowly down the towpath. It seemed to be taking its time, as if it knew it was in control of the situation.

'Oh my God!' blurted out Ash. He was panic-stricken. 'Come on, let's go!' And he began to move off.

But Hudson pulled him back. He watched as the distant figure suddenly stopped and crouched, the seagulls still hovering above its head, some diving and pecking at its hat.

It was about two hundred metres away – too far to see its facial features, but Hudson could just make out the dull blue glow around its shape.

Mokee Joe.

And then, to Hudson's horror, without any warning the figure straightened up and started sprinting towards them.

'*Run! Now!* Down to the old brickworks!'

Ash, normally so particular about packing up his fishing tackle, seemed to have forgotten all about it as the three friends sped off down the towpath.

Hudson ran his fastest and Molly, as usual, was even faster; but neither of them could keep up with Ash, who was the first to leap through the doorway of the disused brick factory. They all took cover in the shadows, hiding in a corner among the dust and rubble, waiting, listening for any signs of pursuit. But all was quiet.

And then Hudson's blood froze as a silhouette glided slowly into view outside the window. Molly stifled a scream and Ash breathed heavily.

'Keep still and don't make a sound,' Hudson whispered.

The dark shape moved on and disappeared, but seconds later, an elongated shadow appeared in the doorway. It hovered there, and it was obvious to the terrified trio that it was looking and listening for signs of life. Hudson saw the eerie blue glow surrounding it and heard a faint crackling sound – like bacon frying in a pan, but much less welcoming.

And then the shadowy face turned and seemed to stare in.

Hudson knew it couldn't see him and he stared back, trying desperately to decipher its features. He thought he could just about detect the outline of a mouth and nose, but though he could sense the intensity of its stare, the eyes remained invisible.

He concentrated, emptying his mind of all thoughts.

He felt sure that the looming shape was trying to pick up his thought waves.

Finally, to everyone's immense relief, the figure glided away.

'Has he gone?' Ash whimpered.

'I think so,' Hudson replied. 'But stay still a bit longer – just to be sure.'

'I can't wait much longer,' Molly hissed. 'I need the *loo*!'

And then they heard a series of loud splashes from somewhere outside. Hudson crept towards the window and peered back up the towpath.

'He's sitting by your fishing tackle,' he whispered to Ash.

Ash crept out of the shadows with Molly following. They too leaned out of the window.

'Oh, God! What's he doing?' Ash exclaimed in horror.

They all watched helplessly as Mokee Joe squatted on Ash's fishing box, callously throwing each item of his beloved fishing tackle into the murky water of the canal.

'Where's your mobile?' Hudson asked. 'We need to phone the police!'

'I left it in my fishing box!' Ash wailed, now almost in tears.

A young couple with an Alsatian on a lead suddenly appeared outside the window. Hudson reacted immediately.

'Excuse me!' he shouted, climbing through the gap. Ash and Molly followed. 'That man up there is scaring us. Can you help?'

The young man looked up the towpath and saw what was happening. 'Well of all the . . . !' He freed the dog from its lead and pointed up the towpath. It growled savagely and made a beeline for the squatting figure. At the same time, the young woman took a mobile from her bag and dialled the police.

It seemed to Hudson that things were beginning to swing back in their favour.

But as they watched the dog bear down on its target, the gaunt figure snarled, grabbed the unfortunate animal by the collar, swung it round several times and then flung it into the canal. It surfaced a whimpering bundle of wet fur, but somehow managed to swim to the side, where its stunned owner helped it out.

But more luck was on Hudson's side.

Four members of the Danvers Green Rugby Club came jogging from the opposite direction, out for their regular Sunday afternoon training run. The three friends, along with the young couple, began yelling for help, yet although the men were big enough to deter anyone, the creature didn't seem afraid. Instead, Hudson sensed that it was simply angry at the sudden intrusion, as if this was not part of its plan. It pulled its collar over its face and, for the moment at least, decided to retreat.

Picking up Ash's huge fishing umbrella, the creature turned it upside down and placed it in the canal. Everyone gasped as it climbed in and used it like a boat, paddling with its bony hands to escape to the other side.

'*Hey, come back with my brolly!*' Ash yelled, feeling braver with the small crowd around him.

'I don't believe this!' Molly howled. 'He's going to get away again! The police will never be here in time.'

Hudson thought about Guardian Angel and the word 'mission' came into his head. It was time to act. He had quickly figured out that even the most formidable enemy was a touch vulnerable when balancing on an upturned brolly in a canal – especially when it was seven feet tall and had a high centre of gravity. Without a word, he kicked off his shoes, ran up the towpath and dived in.

'*Hudson, what d'you think you're doing?*' Molly screamed after him.

'I'm going to tip him over,' Hudson spluttered as he came to the surface. 'I've just got a feeling he doesn't like water.'

Hudson was a strong swimmer and it only took him a few strokes to reach the upturned brolly. But as he tried to grab hold of it, the creature reached into one of its grubby raincoat pockets and produced a stout iron bar.

'Hudson, *watch out!*' Molly yelled. 'He's got a weapon!'

Hudson stopped swimming and looked up at the awful figure towering above him. The faint blue glow still surrounded it and Hudson could hear the sound of electricity crackling from its fingers into the metal. With a show of incredible strength, it bent the bar until the ends were almost touching. Behind him, Hudson heard his small audience gasp in disbelief.

'Get out of the way, lad!' one of the Rugby Club members shouted. 'You haven't a chance – he'll split your skull!'

'Yes, Hudson!' Molly joined in. 'Get away! I've got a better idea!'

Hudson turned and saw Molly with a large brick in her hands. He started swimming back towards her, the creature paddling furiously after him.

Molly ran towards the water and threw the brick with all her might. Just in time, Hudson turned to see the heavy missile land inside the brolly, causing it to rock wildly from side to side.

'Well done, lass!' one of the joggers shouted encouragingly. 'That's slowed him!'

'Wow! Brilliant!' Hudson puffed as he heaved himself out of the canal.

'*Come on!*' Molly demanded. 'Somebody help me!'

There were lots of broken bricks lying around outside the old factory, and Ash and the Rugby Club joggers were quick to realise what Molly wanted them to do.

The creature had now sailed close to the nearest bank and it was quite easy to hurl the heavy bricks at its feet. One after the other, the missiles rained down into the umbrella so that it sank lower and lower into the water.

'Keep going!' Molly shouted. 'We've got him!'

Hudson sat exhausted on the towpath and watched as, yet again, the tables turned in his favour. He could sense the creature's confusion as it wobbled precariously and tried frantically to paddle back to the other side.

'The brolly's about to capsize!' someone yelled.

The biggest of the Rugby Club members hurled a huge brick towards the retreating umbrella. It was a direct hit and as it found its mark, sure enough, the brolly went over and its grim occupant hit the water.

A loud bang echoed down the canal, followed by a blinding flash of light. Swirls of smoke rose up from the water. Hudson fell onto his back, his legs waving in the air.

Molly ran over and helped him up. The two of them looked out onto the canal and waited for the dense, foul-smelling clouds to clear.

'Hudson, what's happened? D'you think we've killed him?'

Hudson stood there, sodden and shivering. 'I don't know.'

Ash ran up to them, followed by the joggers, and finally the young couple with the dog. They all squinted out at the water.

Slowly, the smoke cleared.

'What the hell's happened?' one of the joggers cried.

'Oh my God!' the young woman gasped, putting her hands to her face.

Ash simply drew a sharp breath.

Hudson and Molly surveyed the scene in front of them. The entire surface of the canal was oily black and littered with dead fish. Ash's fishing umbrella was still floating upside down, but now it was just a wire skeleton with all the covering burnt away. Other items of fishing tackle bobbed, blackened, in the water and two dead ducks, charred and featherless, drifted amongst the wreckage.

But there was no sign of Mokee Joe.

A distant police siren sounded as Hudson took Molly aside. 'I don't know what just happened here, but I know the battle's not over by a long way.'

'What d'you mean?' she whispered in his ear. 'Surely that *thing*'s gone for ever? It can't have survived that?'

Hudson looked up the towpath towards the iron bridge and as Molly followed his gaze, she gulped in disbelief.

There, standing in the middle of the bridge, was the sinister figure. It looked darker than usual and smoke appeared to be rising from its hat.

But it was still very much alive and Hudson and Molly watched in horror as it waved defiantly at them before turning on its heels.

Finally, Hudson felt his wet sleeve being pulled sharply and heard Molly's desperate voice in his ear.

'Hudson – can we go now? I really *do* need the loo!'

6

BACK to SchOOL

Despite it being Monday morning, Hudson's least favourite time of the week, he felt a sense of relief. Back to school meant back to some sort of normality.

At half-past eight, he met Molly by her gate and they walked along Byron Road towards Danvers Green Primary. Hudson was jumpy and kept looking back over his shoulder.

'D'you think he's watching us?' Molly asked.

'It wouldn't surprise me,' Hudson answered. 'In fact, I don't think anything'll ever surprise me again. Guardian Angel watches me, so why not Mokee Joe?'

'Well, don't you worry, I'll protect you!' enthused Molly. 'I was practising my latest judo moves last night. I gave Sampson absolute hell. Mum came up the stairs twice to find out what all the banging was about and when she found me rolling around the floor with him in a headlock, she threatened to report me to the RSPCA!'

Hudson laughed. He could just imagine Molly and her playful golden Labrador wrestling on the floor. The dog adored Molly and would let her do whatever she wanted.

'Hey, no laughing – I take my judo very seriously,' Molly warned, pretending to be annoyed. And before Hudson knew what was happening, he found himself caught in that famous headlock.

'Let go!' Hudson's muffled cry came from under the tight grip of her arm. 'You'll ruin my hair!'

Molly let go and pushed him away. 'Oh, sorry!' she said mockingly. 'Don't want to spoil the hair, do we?' She straightened her jumper, smoothed down her skirt, then grew more serious. 'So, come on, who d'you think this Mokee Joe is, and where does he come from?'

Hudson frowned as he scanned the passers-by. 'Search me. He's like some sort of – I don't know – terminator. But what I really want to know is, why is he—?'

Suddenly, from out of nowhere, a tall figure in a long raincoat with upturned collar, holding onto a hat, came running towards them.

Molly clutched Hudson's arm and screamed, 'HUDSON, LOOK OUT!'

But it was too late – the advancing figure was already upon them. As it reached Molly, she charged against it with all her might, using the full force of her shoulder to throw it off balance. It hit the pavement and rolled over.

'*Oi! What in the—?*'

Hudson looked down at the man's startled face with

its bushy beard, then at Molly's embarrassed expression. He burst out laughing.

'I hardly think Mokee Joe's grown a beard overnight!'

They helped the poor man to his feet and apologised. No, no, he said, it was he who should be sorry for alarming them, but he was rushing to try and catch the number 17 bus from the corner of the High Street.

As soon as the man had gone, Hudson started laughing again.

'It's not funny!' Molly snapped. 'What if that *had* been Mokee Joe. We would never have got away, would we?'

Hudson looked serious again. As usual, Molly was absolutely right and the sooner they got to school and into the safety of the playground, the better.

Passing through the school gates, the two friends breathed a sigh of relief. It was true that there was safety in numbers.

Ash was waiting for them. 'Hi, you guys! What's happening?'

Hudson was still looking over his shoulder and beyond the railings. 'Nothing much,' he answered. 'Are you OK?'

'Yeah, I'm OK. But when I got home last night, my dad went ballistic!'

'I'm not surprised,' Molly chipped in, 'you arriving home in a police car!'

'Yes – and without my fishing tackle and my mobile,' Ash added sadly. His eyes opened wide as he recalled the events of the previous evening. 'Anyway, at least Dad had insured them, so I'll get them replaced.'

'Well that's one good thing,' Hudson said, giving his friend an affectionate punch.

Ash grinned. 'The look on those policemen's faces was a picture, wasn't it? I still don't think they really believed anyone about the umbrella capsizing and the big bang and everything.'

'You can hardly blame them really, can you?' Molly added, checking through her schoolbag. 'By the way, I nearly forgot. I found this last night. Have a look.'

She passed a piece of paper over to Hudson. It was a cutting from the Danvers Green Advertiser. He and Ash looked at the bold headline.

'CHILDREN TERRORISED IN KILN STREET AREA'.

'Wow! If I'd known about this,' Ash said, 'I would never have gone fishing up there.'

Hudson read on: *'Police have received complaints regarding a number of incidents in and around Danvers Green. Recent reports have involved a suspicious figure chasing and harassing children along the towpath of the Danvers and Dearne Canal. The man has been described as tall and scruffily dressed – possibly a tramp – and he should not be approached under any circumstances.'*

'So it's *not* just you, Hudson!' Molly said. 'Seems he's stalking loads of kids.'

'She's right,' Ash added, his eyes wide again. 'He's just a crazy guy that gets his kicks creeping along the canal and causing trouble. Though I still don't know how on earth he got through on my mobile.'

Hudson shook his head and looked from Molly to Ash, then back to Molly again.

'It's not that simple, Ash,' Molly said, reading Hudson's thoughts. 'I don't think Mokee Joe's just some crazy guy. He's more like something out of a horror film. You don't know the half of it.'

Ash went quiet, put his hands in his pockets and stared thoughtfully at the ground.

Before anyone could say anything else, the bell signalled the beginning of lessons and they moved off in silence towards the school building.

The lesson before morning break was science. Hudson gazed down dreamily at the textbook on his desk, which showed a drawing of a boy throwing a ball into the air and the words 'kinetic energy' written underneath. He looked up at the teacher, old Mr Trueman, who was droning on about energy in all its different forms and was just about to start making notes on the whiteboard.

'Sir!' Hudson shouted, putting his hand up. 'What does "kinetic" mean?'

Mr Trueman swivelled round to face the class. Despite the fact that his spectacles had extra thick lenses, everyone knew he was as blind as a bat.

'Well, it's funny you should ask that, Geoffrey, because I was going to talk about kinetic energy after break.'

'Sir – I'm not Geoffrey, I'm Hudson.'

The whole class giggled.

'Oh yes! Well, Hudson,' the teacher bumbled on, 'the word "kinetic" means "movement". Hence, kinetic energy is energy due to movement.'

Hudson nodded, making a few notes at the same time.

'And what about the initials MO, Sir? Do they mean anything?'

Hudson could sense the other pupils looking curiously at him.

'Strange question, Hudson! I'm not sure what it's got to do with our lesson.' Mr Trueman looked thoughtful and scratched his head. 'The only MO I can think of is in MOD – Ministry of Defence. Why do you ask?'

'Oh, it's OK, Sir,' Hudson replied, sounding pleased with himself. 'It's just something I've been reading about at home.'

'Well in that case, let's get on with the lesson and stop wasting time. Now can anyone see where I put my board marker?'

Hudson looked across at Molly. He could see by her face that she knew he was onto something. But she would have to wait until break to find out what it was.

At 11.15, morning break finally arrived. It was raining outside so the children hung around in the corridor.

'Well?' Molly asked impatiently. 'What was all that about with old Trueman? You've found something out, haven't you?'

Sipping his orange juice, Hudson stared at Molly's freckles. She had identical clusters on each cheek, which reminded him of star constellations. Hudson was really into star constellations. In fact, lately he'd been getting into everything to do with space and stars and stuff like that. The night sky fascinated him and he'd started reading books on astronomy from the school library at every opportunity. Molly joked that he probably came from another planet, he was so obsessed by them.

'Yes – the MOK in "Mokee" stands for Ministry of Kinetics.' A loud, rasping sound signified his carton was empty.

'How do you know that?' Molly asked, sounding impressed and frustrated at the same time.

'I just do!' he answered firmly, as if that was explanation enough. 'Question is, what do "EE" and "Joe" mean?'

'If we knew that, then I suppose we might know who or what Mokee Joe is, and maybe even where he comes from,' Molly added, beginning to sound enthusiastic.

'Exactly! And when we know what we're dealing with—' Hudson suddenly stopped. Molly was giving him one of her challenging stares. '*What?*'

'You're really beginning to enjoy this, Hudson, aren't you? It's all turning into a game!' She pulled the straw out from her empty carton and flicked the end of it so that several drops of apple juice landed on the end of Hudson's nose. Then she frowned at him, but Hudson detected another look behind the frown. Admiration?

Hudson felt a blush coming on. 'I'm just playing along, that's all,' he said, squashing his orange carton flat with both hands.

'Well, just remember, it's not really a game,' Molly said firmly. 'From what we've seen, it's far more serious than that.'

Molly was, of course, absolutely right. Really, she could be so sensible at times!

The bell sounded again and they went off for the second part of their science lesson. Science was one of Hudson's favourite subjects. He found it interesting and fun, and he was good at it. Normally, he would have been concentrating and writing furiously, but today his mind kept wandering.

He was thinking back to the canal incident, especially that big bang and the blinding flash when Mokee Joe had hit the water. *Electricity does that when it comes into contact with water*, Hudson thought to himself. He remembered a murder scene in a film where someone had thrown an electric fire into a bath, with similar results. The person in the bath had been killed, just like the fish in the canal.

He was remembering the blue glow surrounding Mokee Joe's hands when he felt something strike his right ear. A small rolled-up piece of paper landed on his desk. Hudson looked straight at Molly and sure enough, she was trying to attract his attention. Her face wore a horrified expression and the colour had drained from her cheeks. She looked at him pleadingly and then stared in the direction of the window. Hudson followed her gaze, out across the playground, and gasped.

Leaning nonchalantly on the school railings and staring back at him was the tall spectre of Mokee Joe.

Hudson had been rolling a pencil between his fingers. When he saw the creature across the yard he squeezed it so tight that it suddenly snapped with a loud CRACK.

'Are you OK?' asked the boy sitting next to him.

Hudson turned to him, but before he could answer, a loud din sounded from outside.

CLANG-CLANG-CLANG-CLANG!

Now everyone was peering out of the window as the sinister figure rattled an iron bar along the railings. The only person who didn't react was Mr Trueman, who, as well as being short-sighted, was hard of hearing.

As the terrible row continued, the whole class left their seats and went over to the window. A frail and feeble boy called Bertie Small hid behind everyone and began to cry.

Hudson, Molly and the others watched with a mixture

of unease and fascination as the angular form strutted up and down, making its defiant racket. Each time the bar struck the railings, a bright blue spark danced into the air.

The teacher scribbled away on the board, completely unaware of the scene behind him.

'Hudson, what are we going to do?' Molly whispered.

'I think somebody should phone the police,' he replied, his gaze fixed firmly on Mokee Joe.

At that moment, Mr Trueman swung round and was amazed to see his entire class gathered round the window.

'What's happened?' he cried. 'Are you all out of your seats? Get back at once!'

The clanging stopped.

Disappointed that the entertainment seemed to be coming to an end, the pupils slouched back to their places. Bertie Small stopped crying and started blowing his nose.

Hudson called out loudly, 'Sir, there's a suspicious man outside and I think someone should phone the police!'

The short-sighted teacher walked over to the window and looked out. 'What man? I can't see anyone!'

Hudson looked again. The creature was back in its original position, leaning on the railings and staring, without seeming to, in Hudson's direction.

While Mr Trueman removed his glasses and started wiping them, Hudson looked at Molly and, with his head, indicated the door. Knowing what he wanted her to do, she got up and sneaked out into the corridor.

The teacher replaced his thick-rimmed spectacles. 'Look! I've had just about enough of this!' he barked. 'This is a conspiracy designed to waste time. Well, it won't work! Any more nonsense and I'll keep everyone in at break.' He looked over at Hudson. 'I'm surprised at you, Geoffrey. I thought you would have known better!'

The rest of the class sighed as Mr Trueman tried to continue his lesson, but no-one could concentrate. All eyes were firmly glued to the silhouette outside.

Out of the corner of his eye, Hudson saw Molly slip back through the door and into her seat, just in time to see the creature's next trick. A gasp echoed around the room as Mokee Joe took hold of two of the railings and forced them apart.

'Wow! He did that as easy as if they were made of plasticine!' the boy next to Hudson whispered in awe.

Bertie Small began to cry again.

But Hudson wasn't listening. He knew the show was for his benefit and his eyes remained fixed on the creature as it threatened to climb through the wide gap. But it didn't. It just stood there, motionless and more menacing than ever.

A few minutes later a police siren sounded and Hudson smiled over at Molly. But glancing back to the railings he could only watch in frustration as the gaunt figure slouched away, waving its arms in defiance, always one step ahead, it seemed.

And then it was gone.

The police car pulled up and two men in uniform got out. They took a quick look round, then walked through the school gates. Hudson glanced back to Molly and saw that she appeared distinctly nervous. As the policemen walked across the yard, the whole of 6T started buzzing.

About five minutes later, a knock sounded on the

classroom door. One of the younger pupils came in with a note and passed it to Mr Trueman. He read it, signed it and turned to face the class.

'If I can have your attention for a minute,' he began. 'It seems that Mr Fletcher would like to see everyone in the Assembly Hall straight after lunch at 1.15.'

Hudson looked across at Molly and could see that she was even more anxious than before. He hated to see his best friend looking like this. The sooner it got to lunch-time the better.

During lunch, Ash had been filled in about all that had happened during the morning. He'd listened wide-eyed as usual, but still managed to devour a full plate of sausage, chips and beans.

'Wow! I wish I'd been there,' he mumbled through a mouthful of food. 'Our maths lesson was totally boring. It seems this Mokee Joe character is really out to get you, Hudson.'

Molly cheekily took one of Ash's last remaining chips and stared at it between her fingers before eating it slowly. 'That's just what Hudson wants to hear, Ash,' she said sarcastically. 'You really know how to cheer a guy up.'

'I'd like to suggest that we hold an emergency meeting in Candleshed at seven o'clock this evening,' Hudson stated in his most formal voice. 'We need to discuss everything that's happened and decide what our next step should be.'

'Agreed,' replied Molly.

'Agreed,' Ash added, though he didn't look too comfortable.

'Come on,' Hudson said. 'Let's get some fresh air and

check out the playground before we meet up with old Fletcher.'

Molly's face went ashen at the mention of the headmaster. She'd forgotten about that for a moment. Without saying a word, she put the half-eaten chip back on Ash's plate and got up to leave.

One-fifteen found Hudson and his two friends sitting in the front row of the Assembly Hall anxiously awaiting the arrival of the headmaster. Hudson noticed that Molly was unusually quiet.

Mr Fletcher finally walked in, accompanied by a policeman with three stripes on his arm. Both men looked serious.

'Now, children,' the headmaster began, 'one of you made a call to the police this morning and wasted their valuable time. I would very much like to know who that person was.'

Hudson looked straight at Molly and saw that she was biting her bottom lip. He felt sorry for her.

'If no-one owns up,' Mr Fletcher continued, 'then I shall be forced to cancel the school visits planned over the term, and that includes the Year Six outing to Macalisters Biscuit Factory scheduled for tomorrow.'

Mutterings of dissent sounded around the hall. The policeman stood with his hands behind his back, rocking on his heels and looking grave. Mr Fletcher was well aware how much they had all been looking forward to their Humanities trip. Macalisters was popular, to say the least, and a rumour had gone round that they would be allowed a sampling session during the tour.

But just as Hudson had decided to take the blame

himself, a familiar voice, strong but rather shaky, piped up by his side.

'It was me, Sir!' Molly called out. 'But I wasn't wasting anyone's time. We really needed the police, Sir – you can ask anyone in 6T.'

'That's true,' Hudson added. 'There was this man—'

'OK, OK,' the police sergeant interrupted, folding his arms. 'It sounds like we can get to the bottom of this, Mr Fletcher.'

Mr Fletcher delivered a brief lecture on the proper procedure for contacting the emergency services at school and then 6T were told to stay behind as the rest of the school were dismissed.

Five minutes later, the headmaster and the sergeant listened intently as Hudson gave a blow-by-blow account of all that had happened over the past few days and Molly chipped in from time to time for effect. The rest of 6T confirmed the strange events in the playground and Ash, who'd also stayed behind, told the policeman all about his lost fishing tackle.

'What we have here,' the sergeant finally said, 'is a case of a tramp or down-and-out causing bother and frightening children. The police are already aware of this man and are doing their best to catch him. He may be quite harmless, but we'll all need to be on our guard. Mr Fletcher will speak to the school again and your parents will be contacted and made aware of the situation. In future, if you see anything suspicious around the school, you must report it straight to a member of staff.'

'Which is exactly what we did,' Hudson and Molly muttered to each other.

As the children were leaving, Hudson stared across at the sergeant and caught him staring back. The policeman looked distinctly uncomfortable and quickly turned away. Now Hudson was sure the man knew more than he was letting on.

After school, Hudson met up with Molly. They made their way cautiously to the school gate and double-checked that Mokee Joe was nowhere to be seen. Then they ran most of the way home without talking. Hudson said they should save any further discussion for their seven o'clock meeting and get indoors as soon as possible.

He left Molly by her gate. 'See you at seven!' he called. 'And get a lift from your mum, OK?'

A few minutes later, Hudson was jogging up Tennyson Road towards number 13. He kept looking over his shoulder and even found himself peering over the privet hedges lining the road, wondering if his enemy was lying in wait for him. Finally, as he approached the garden gate, he saw that someone was sitting on the doorstep. It was a young boy and as Hudson drew nearer, he had to look twice to check he wasn't dreaming.

The boy had the same hot-cross-bun hairstyle as himself. In fact, his features were exactly the same. A little younger perhaps, but same face, same eyes, same expression. He was wearing a kind of all-white tracksuit and his shoes were sparkling silver, with no laces.

'Hi – who are you?' Hudson asked.

The boy looked up at him blankly and Hudson noted a sadness in his eyes.

'I don't know,' he replied.

'Well, where are you from and why are you sitting there?'

'I don't know.'

'Do you know anything?' Hudson asked sympathetically.

'No! My mind is completely blank. I'm frightened!'

Hudson felt sorry for the young boy. 'You'd better come in,' he said.

As the boy stood up, Hudson noticed a label of some kind stitched into his tracksuit top where the breast pocket should have been. He looked closer and his eyes grew wide as he read the letters HUD-SON.

And then a loud bang from around the side of the house distracted him. It sounded like dustbins falling over.

'Don't move,' he ordered the boy. 'I'll be back in a second.'

There was a narrow passage between Hudson's house and the neighbours at number 15, and two dustbins were kept there. Creeping carefully into the alleyway, he found them both on their sides, the contents scattered on the ground.

Looking around nervously, he cleared up the mess and stood them upright again. He was wondering what could have knocked them over when he spotted an object amongst the rubbish.

The sight of it struck terror in his heart.

It was an iron bar – *that* iron bar, still bent from Mokee Joe's demonstration at the canal and no doubt the same one he'd dragged along the railings.

Running back round to the front of the house, Hudson shouted to the young boy to go inside, but he was gone – vanished.

Hudson's mind swam around in confusion. Everything was getting unreal again.

He opened the front door. A warm, reassuring voice greeted him.

'Hudson! Is that you? Tea's almost ready. Go and wash your hands.'

His mum's voice sounded so comforting and then the gorgeous smell of spag bol wafted down the hallway and greeted his nostrils. It was his favourite meal, and he was usually ravenous for it. But his appetite wasn't quite as hearty today. He couldn't stop thinking about that sad little boy with the sad little face, sitting there on the doorstep. The thought of him made Hudson want to cry.

Then he smelt the food again and, in spite of himself, he began to feel a bit hungrier. He licked his lips and prayed that it was real.

7

Stuff of Nightmares

It was seven o'clock and down in Candleshed, Hudson was telling Molly and Ash about the boy on the doorstep and the disturbance around the dustbins. He explained exactly what had happened, relishing the amazement on Molly and Ash's faces.

'And then he just disappeared,' Hudson concluded in dramatic fashion.

'Into thin air?' Molly asked, her big eyes shining in the gloom.

'Yes!'

'Who do you think he was?' Ash asked.

Hudson scratched his chin and said, 'I don't know.'

But secretly, he suspected that he'd seen a vision of himself – some sort of flashback to his past.

Molly interrupted his thoughts. 'What's this got to do with Mokee Joe?'

Hudson shrugged his shoulders. 'I don't know that either.'

'What do you think we should do next?' Ash whispered.

Hudson said nothing. Molly and Ash looked at him expectantly.

'I could try to contact GA,' he said after a moment.

'Oh, so it's not strictly one-way?' Molly asked.

'What are you two talking about?' Ash asked with a puzzled look on his face. 'Who's GA?'

'I can't explain now, Ash,' Hudson replied. 'Just hang on while I try something. Molly – remember what happened over that shopping list for the Castle?' She nodded. 'I'm going to try and concentrate on a candle and see if anything comes to me.'

Molly lit the candle in the centre of the table. Hudson poised himself over a piece of paper with a pencil at the ready. He focused all his attention on the flickering flame, hoping he wouldn't find himself drifting up to the shed roof.

Molly and Ash watched expectantly.

Everything seemed to go very quiet. The darkness intensified and a wind suddenly whipped up outside. Raindrops began to tap on the windows and somewhere in the distance, a dog howled.

After a moment, Hudson's eyes began to change. The pupils grew large. And then his writing hand began to tremble.

'I don't like this,' Ash whispered in a frightened voice.

'Sshh,' Molly muttered. 'He knows what he's doing.'

Hudson's eyes remained fixed on the candle. He felt his hand begin to write, even though he hadn't moved it. He tried to speak but his mouth wouldn't let him.

Molly gasped as the words appeared on the paper. 'Hudson?'

He still couldn't speak. His hand continued to move but he had no idea what he was writing.

All of a sudden, the candle went out.

'HUDSON!' Molly yelled.

Hudson strained to move but he was frozen.

'Hey, I *definitely* don't like this!' Ash cried, heading for the door. His chair went crashing over.

'This isn't funny!' Molly said desperately, searching for the matches.

Hudson continued to struggle against the strange force that had taken over his body. It was an odd feeling, but he knew it was only Guardian Angel and that he wouldn't be harmed. He tensed and willed his helper to let him go.

And then he was himself again. Guardian Angel had left him. He shivered, even though it wasn't cold.

The door of the shed flapped open and he could hear Ash's hurried steps running away down the path. A flickering light appeared as Molly relit the candle.

Hudson looked across at her. 'I-I don't know w-what happened,' he stammered.

'Just sit still and relax,' Molly said calmly, as she picked up Ash's overturned chair.

She lit two more candles and placed them in the centre of the table. Hudson leaned over and looked at the words that had appeared on the piece of paper.

'13 Kiln Street'

'That's down by the old brickworks, isn't it?' Molly asked.

'Yes, I think so,' Hudson agreed. 'It's near where we all were on Sunday. We've got to go there and investigate as soon as possible.'

Hudson saw Molly's face change. She looked determined – almost excited at the prospect.

'How about tomorrow, straight after school?' he asked.

'Yes, that's OK, but don't forget I have my judo class at seven so we mustn't be too long.'

'I've just been thinking,' Hudson suddenly added. 'Aren't most of those houses empty?'

A voice from outside the door startled them and Molly almost jumped out of her seat.

It was Ash, grinning sheepishly around the door. 'Most of them are,' he offered, 'but a few are still lived in. Lots of them were closed up when the factory shut down.'

Molly stood up and folded her arms across her chest. 'And what happened to you?' she pouted.

'Sorry, Mol – I just panicked when the light went out. I can't stand the dark.'

'Don't worry,' said Hudson, 'it's no big deal.' He showed Ash the strange message. 'I don't suppose you want to go up there tomorrow with me and Molly?'

'No thanks, I'll give it a miss. But you two take care. Those houses are spooky. Even the ones that are lived in are really run down, and there are some dodgy characters living up there.'

Hudson glanced at Molly. She was biting her lip and looking more determined than ever. 'OK, thanks for the warning – we'll be extra careful,' he said.

'Well, I'll be off now if you don't mind,' Ash said, sounding as if he'd had enough excitement for one night. 'E-mail me when you get back tomorrow night. I'm dying to know how it works out.'

'Ash – say that again!' Hudson said mysteriously.

Ash and Molly looked puzzled. 'I just asked if you'd e-mail me tomorrow night,' said Ash.

'OK. Now tell me – what does the "e" stand for in "e-mail"?'

Before Ash could reply, Molly spoke up for him. 'It stands for "electronic", as in "electronic mail",' she said dismissively. 'Everyone knows *that*!'

Hudson took the piece of paper again and scribbled on it. He held it up to Molly and Ash. He'd written the word 'MOKEE' in big letters.

'What's all this?' Ash asked.

'Ministry Of Kinetics, Electronic . . . but I don't know what the other "e" or the "Joe" mean yet.'

'But why "electronic"?' asked Ash, clearly baffled.

'Well, there's the blue light, and something electronic would cause a bang if it came into contact with water,' Hudson said in a matter-of-fact way. 'It's all coming together. I'm sure we're going to get to the bottom of this Mokee Joe creature sooner or later.'

Hudson looked at the faces of his two closest friends. Ash was completely bewildered, and even Molly was looking a bit confused. He could see that as far as they were concerned, it would definitely be later rather than sooner.

That night, Hudson was walking down Tennyson Road towards Molly's when suddenly he found, to his horror, that Mokee Joe was chasing him. Some way ahead, he could see Molly and Ash, a policeman and Mr Fletcher. He could also just make out his parents. They were all screaming at him to run faster, and he knew that if he could reach them in time, he would be safe. But his legs seemed to be slowing down.

Looking back over his shoulder, he saw the shadowy form gaining on him. As the creature drew closer, its long, scrawny arms and bony fingers reached out to grab hold of him.

His would-be rescuers were now screaming louder than ever, especially Molly, but the more they beckoned him, the heavier and wearier his legs grew.

Now he seemed to be running in slow motion and without turning round, he could sense that he was almost caught. His legs turned to jelly and he started to fall. He looked in desperation towards Molly and Ash . . . *but they had all disappeared!* Now his entire body refused to move and he crashed to the ground, rolling onto his back to face his attacker.

Mokee Joe stopped at his feet and loomed over him.

Hudson stared upwards in horror. His enemy now appeared to be at least ten feet tall. The monster slowly crouched down until it was kneeling over his waist, pinning him to the floor and staring down into his face. As the creature raised its arms and started beating on Hudson's chest like a drum, first with one fist, then the other, Hudson was sure he was going to die.

But surprisingly, the pounding didn't hurt and he started to think that perhaps Mokee Joe wasn't as strong as he appeared. Then, as if the creature could read his mind, it suddenly stopped beating him. Hudson lay helpless, the monster kneeling menacingly over him.

Everything was bathed in a blue glow, the air charged with electricity. Hudson's whole body tingled and his hair was alive with static.

Then the fiend leaned forward so that its face was only inches away from Hudson's. Hudson could see his enemy's hideous features in every detail, he could even smell its foul breath – a sort of stale, oily odour. Gazing into its black, beady eyes, he was aware of the tiny, piercing pupils penetrating his own, as if trying to read his thoughts. All around the sickly grey face were dotted metal studs, each about the size and colour of a one-penny piece. Then the creature's thin black lips parted to reveal needle-sharp, jagged teeth. It leaned in close and opened wide. Hudson braced himself, terror-stricken, ready – this time, surely – for the end.

What happened next was almost as bad.

As the vile creature moved even closer, it flicked out its long, snake-like tongue and began to lick Hudson's nose. This shocked him so much that he screamed a long piercing scream . . .

And then woke up.

Pugwash had come in through the open bedroom window and was standing on Hudson's chest, padding his front paws on Hudson's pyjama jacket and licking his face at the same time.

As soon as he saw his furry friend, Hudson breathed an immense sigh of relief and started to chuckle to himself. It had all been a terrible nightmare. No creature could be that hideous. And yet it had all seemed so real! Too real! Hudson had a horrible feeling that Mokee Joe had somehow got into his head – like Guardian Angel.

He sat up and gently placed the cat on the floor. 'Pugwash, thank God it's only you,' he whispered.

He got out of bed and went over to the bedroom window to close it. As he did, he couldn't resist leaning out and looking up at the night sky. It was clear and he gazed in wonder at the sea of twinkling stars. They never failed to fascinate him.

As always, one particular star pattern attracted his attention. He knew the name of it – 'Orion', sometimes known as 'the Hunter'. He looked at each star in its formation and then at the one that glowed bigger and brighter than the rest. It was situated on the Hunter's shoulder, and always he was drawn to look at it, as if it had some special significance for him. He just didn't know what – yet.

Hudson came back down to Earth as Pugwash began meowing behind him.

'What is it? Do you want to go out again?'

He lifted the cat onto the window ledge, but Pugwash began to hiss and all his fur stood on end. When he put the cat back on the floor, it scuttled under the bed and refused to come out.

And then a terrifying thought entered Hudson's mind.

He returned to the window and leaned out again. But this time, instead of looking up, he looked down. And sure enough, beyond the side of the house, he could just discern a big shadow on the neighbour's wall.

It was an ominous, crouching shadow, lurking between the dustbins like a giant rat. Hudson knew at once it was his enemy, stalking and waiting. Butterflies began to flutter wildly in his stomach.

What to do?

He looked at the clock on his bedside cabinet. It was just after midnight. The house was quiet except for Mr Brown's heavy snoring coming from the next bedroom.

Hudson looked out again. The shadow was still there.

Plucking up all his courage, he decided to sneak downstairs and go out to investigate. A few moments later, he opened the front door and looked out. The street was deserted. Creeping towards the side of the house, his heart started thumping as he detected a scurrying movement from the passageway.

But then suddenly there were other sounds.

Hudson turned and saw three men approaching from up the road. Singing at the tops of their voices, they had their arms around each other and were staggering slightly – late night revellers who'd had too much to drink.

Hudson shouted across the road.

'Eh . . . excuse me . . . excuse me! There's a man hiding between these houses! Could you get rid of him? He's keeping me awake and giving me nightmares!'

Hudson pointed to where the shadow was. It had now stopped moving.

One of the men, the biggest, immediately started across the road. 'Is that right, son? Well, we'll sort him out,' he slurred, full of confidence and fighting spirit.

'No problem!' one of his friends joined in. Before long, all three of them had swaggered across the road and disappeared into the dark gap between the houses.

Hudson hoped he wasn't leading his rescuers into danger. He remembered how easily the creature had bent the iron bar and tackled the Alsatian. But surely it could not take on three huge men, who were full of bravado and temporarily afraid of nothing.

There followed an enormous row and the sound of dustbins clanging and banging in the alleyway. Hudson thought it sounded like a full-scale armoured battle. Heads began to poke through bedroom windows and a man further down the street shouted, '*What the hell's going on?*'

More crashes from the passageway and then the sound of terrible groans before everything finally went quiet.

Finding another reserve of courage, Hudson crept towards the entrance to the alleyway and slowly turned the corner. He shone his torch over the upturned dustbins and his beam picked out the prostrate bodies of the three men. They lay there battered and bruised, moaning in pain.

The biggest of them looked up at Hudson in dismay. His mouth was bloodied and one of his eyes was half shut.

'How many were they?' the man asked him. 'I thought you said there was only one – it was more like an army! For God's sake, phone an ambulance!'

A short while later, a police car arrived followed by an ambulance and the three victims were taken off to hospital. No-one knocked on Hudson's door or asked any awkward questions. He guessed that the police had simply put the incident down to 'drunken behaviour'. Miraculously, his parents had slept through the whole thing and Mr Brown was still snoring as a stunned Hudson made his way back to bed.

He asked himself what sort of creature could put three grown men into hospital so quickly. But then he'd always known that Mokee Joe wasn't just any creature. He was a monster with a mission – to destroy Hudson.

But why?

Hudson yawned and noticed that Pugwash was still cowering under the bed. He walked back to his open bedroom window and took one last look out. The weather had drawn a veil of clouds over his beloved stars. Suddenly he felt sad and alone.

He turned his gaze downwards. A large shadow was silhouetted against the neighbour's wall again – the same crouching, lurking shadow.

Like a giant rat.

8

Into the Lions' Den

Hudson's eyes rolled back as the gentle bumping of the coach lulled him to sleep. The Year Six pupils were on their way to Macalisters Biscuit Factory on the outskirts of Danvers Green. Hudson, Molly and Ash were sitting on the long seat at the back.

'Hudson, you look absolutely shattered!' Molly said.

He looked at her through half-closed eyes. 'I had a bad night,' he answered, yawning.

He told Molly and Ash about Mokee Joe and the incident with the three drunks. 'And when I did eventually get back to bed,' he continued, 'every time I got off to sleep I had a nightmare.'

'What sort of nightmare?' Ash asked, his eyes wide.

'I was being chased by Mokee Joe – but I always woke

up just as he was about to catch me. Until the final night-mare!'

'Why, what happened in that?' Molly asked without looking round. She was busy drawing patterns with her finger on the steamed-up window.

'He caught me by one of my wrists and held it so tight he almost broke it! I woke up in agony.'

Ash shivered at the very thought of it. 'Wow! Some dreams can be so real!'

'Too real!' Hudson agreed. He rolled up his left sleeve and showed the deep bruising on his wrist. Ash was speechless, while Molly, ever practical, tried to suggest that he had probably just banged it without realising – though Hudson could see she didn't believe this for a minute. As for Hudson, he was certain that the shadow outside his bedroom window was somehow responsible.

Molly went back to her window canvas and spelt out in big letters 'MOKEE JOE IS A CREEP'. Then, as Ash and Hudson watched, she drew a big cross through it before vigorously rubbing it out with a stubborn look on her pretty face.

The coach rattled on and Hudson felt his eyes rolling back again.

'Hudson, I've been thinking about your trip to Kiln Street,' Ash said, interrupting Hudson's snooze. 'That old brickworks is just the kind of place for Mokee Joe to hang out. It's big and deserted and it could be the perfect hiding place. You'd better be on your guard tonight!'

Hudson forced himself awake. 'I've been thinking about that too,' he replied. 'Every creature has a lair and you're right – it's the perfect place. And yet I don't think so . . .'

'Why not?' Ash said, sounding slightly annoyed. He'd thought his idea was sound.

'Well – it's just that I can sense—'

'Oh, your sixth sense again!' Ash said dismissively. All this mystery was beginning to make him feel tired – and just a little bit left out.

Molly jumped to Hudson's defence. 'His sixth sense is usually right!' she reminded Ash firmly.

Ash couldn't argue with that so he shut up and turned on his portable CD player. Hudson sat back and gently dozed, feeling strangely safe in the knowledge that Molly was there beside him.

Hudson stirred as the coach pulled up outside the gates of the biscuit factory.

Molly nudged him gently. 'Hudson! We're here!'

A security man came over to the driver's window. He said a few words to the driver, pointed in the direction of the Visitors' Reception and the bus moved on towards the car park.

'OK!' Miss Martin shouted down the bus. 'Everybody off and line up ready for a head count.'

Five minutes later, the manager of Macalisters greeted them, led them away to the reception area and began fitting them out with white aprons and hats.

'This is a health and hygiene regulation,' he explained. 'All the employees at Macalisters have to wear them.'

Hudson hardly noticed the pupils laughing and giggling at each other as they paraded around in their new white uniforms. He was too deep in thought.

'Hudson, what's the matter?' Molly smiled at him,

strutting in front of him to show off her finery. 'Don't you think we look funny in these aprons and hats?'

'Mmm, yeah, great,' Hudson said distractedly. 'It's just that there's something bothering me and I'm not sure what it is.'

Molly frowned. 'Come on, Hudson – relax! I know you've got things on your mind, but just try and have fun today. We're safe here, and don't forget, there's the biscuit-tasting to look forward to!'

He smiled a distant smile. 'Yeah, that's true.' But as he looked down at his own apron he started to fiddle with his watch.

Now he knew what was bothering him. It was the aprons and hats – they were all white. The colour . . . something about the colour . . .

Miss Martin lined them up again and did another count. There was a final reminder to be on their best behaviour and then they all moved off to start the tour.

The first building the manager took them to had a large sign above the doorway that said 'ADDITIVES'.

'Now this is where we keep all those nice things that make plain old biscuits so much more tasty and interesting,' he announced with a jovial smile.

Once inside, Hudson began to relax as a wonderful aroma of spices and other delicious ingredients greeted his nostrils.

'This reminds me of our holiday in India,' he could hear Bertie Small saying, 'when we went to a street market selling herbs and spices. The mixture of all the different smells was just like this. It's great, isn't it?'

'Wicked!' Ash whispered. 'It makes your mouth water.'

'Mmm,' Molly agreed.

Hudson would no doubt have been equally impressed, but his mind was still wandering.

The manager led the party deeper into the building.

'Hey, you two,' Ash exclaimed, 'this place is your actual Aladdin's cave!'

Hudson and Molly nodded. They walked round, looking in awe at the huge shelves stacked with different coloured containers of all shapes and sizes. They drooled over the labels: chocolate of every kind imaginable, all kinds of dried fruits, nuts and vanilla. Large jars of brightly-coloured jams were stored on racks that reached up towards the high ceiling, and on wooden pallets perched plump sacks of spices, many of them open. The children were invited to take a pinch from each one to smell and taste.

'Wow, this place is really great,' Molly said, sampling some ground nutmeg. She put some of the granules into her open hand and blew them into Hudson's face. He sneezed, and Ash had hysterics.

Hudson began to cheer up a bit. He grabbed Molly's wrist and gave her the Chinese Torture. She pretended to scream for Miss Martin, but quietly enough that the teacher didn't hear.

But then, looking along the long rows of bags, he had a thought. 'There's something missing and I can't think what it is.'

Molly, busy dipping into another spice sack, retorted, 'There seems to be everything here to me.'

The manager called the children together. 'OK, everyone, it's time to move on. Follow me!'

En route to the next building, from which various interesting noises were emerging, Hudson noticed a police car parked by the side of a high wire fence surrounding the factory. Two policemen were talking to one of the workers as they all examined a large hole in the bottom of the wire mesh.

Hudson's disquiet returned.

A short while later, they approached a building with another sign painted above it: 'PROCESSING PLANT'. A faint hum of machinery sounded from within.

The children all moved towards the huge doorway and stared in, open-mouthed.

'Hey, come and have a look at this!' Ash beckoned to Hudson and Molly.

They peered in.

'This is the hub of our operation,' the manager was saying. 'The biscuits are actually produced here, from start to finish.'

As a wave of hot air hit Hudson's face, he found himself entranced by the scene in front of him.

Large copper tanks and gold-coloured vats adorned the huge factory floor. Silver pipes criss-crossed the ceiling and steam hissed from valves dotted along their length. Other angry noises filled the air, but the workers seemed oblivious as they scurried around like mice in their spotless white uniforms. And everywhere, long conveyor belts carried biscuits of every shape, size and type.

'Hey, this is cool!' Ash suddenly shouted. 'Look at that!' He pointed at a huge golden vat with the word 'TOFFEE' stamped on it in big letters.

The manager laughed. 'Not exactly cool! Toffee and chocolate are kept extremely hot and moving, so that they stay liquefied.' He pointed up to a silver pipe running across the high ceiling. 'That pipe up there carries liquid chocolate at a rate of 150 litres per minute.'

Wow! thought Hudson. *This is some place!* And just for a moment, he managed to put all worrying thoughts out of his head.

The school party wandered round and watched dough being rolled and shaped by machines. They saw the biscuits being cooked in large ovens and breathed in the delicious smells that emerged. They looked on in delight as plain biscuits travelled along conveyor belts and more machines trickled different flavours onto them. They saw people walking around with clipboards, measuring, testing and sampling the biscuits.

'And as we come to the end of our tour,' the manager said, 'you can see the finished biscuits moving along on conveyor belts towards the packing area.'

And yet there's still something missing from all this, Hudson pondered. *Something we haven't seen yet, and I just can't put my finger on it.*

'So there you have it!' the manager concluded, looking at his watch. 'Now, if you'd all like to follow your teacher back towards reception, I'm sure we can arrange a little tasting session for you – that's if you've got time, Miss Martin?'

'We might just have a few minutes to spare,' the teacher teased. 'OK, children – follow on in pairs, as before, and no dawdling!'

Soon Hudson and Molly were back in reception with the rest of Year Six, having the time of their lives. Large boxes of biscuits, labelled 'BROKEN', were laid out on tables and they were tucking in as if they hadn't eaten for a fortnight.

As Hudson munched away on his favourite – a Macalisters Double Cream Whippy Waffle – and sipped an orange squash, he looked through the reception window and out across the factory yard. About a hundred metres away, he spotted an old brick building that he hadn't noticed before. It was a place they'd not visited and Hudson wondered what was inside.

The manager was standing beside him, talking to Miss Martin.

'Excuse me,' Hudson said politely, looking up at the man. 'Could you tell me what's in that building over there?' He pointed out of the window.

'Oh, that's a rather boring place really. It's where we keep one of our most important ingredients – the Flour Room. It's piled high with sacks and sacks of flour.'

Smash! Hudson's glass of squash slipped from his hand, dropped onto the floor and shattered into a thousand pieces.

All eyes turned to look at him.

'Are you OK, Hudson?' Molly asked first.

'Don't worry, lad,' the manager added. 'We'll get it swept up straight away.'

Miss Martin took Hudson outside. She sat him on a little wooden bench and spoke kindly to him. 'Hudson, are you sure you're all right? You've been very quiet ever since we arrived.'

'I'm fine, Miss – just tired. I've not been sleeping well lately and I just went a bit dizzy in there. It felt stuffy.'

'Yes, I know what you mean – there's not much air inside. Anyway, sit here for a wee while and I'll send someone out to keep you company. We'll be leaving in about five minutes.' And she went back inside.

Ash came out, clutching several chunks of biscuit. His mouth was smeared with chocolate.

'Are you OK, Hudson?' he asked, spitting crumbs everywhere as he spoke. 'Miss Martin asked me to keep an eye on you.'

'No, not really. I've just realised where Mokee Joe's hideout is!'

Ash looked puzzled.

'You know – where he hangs out?' Hudson went on. 'His lair – his den.'

'Wicked!' Ash replied, munching happily. But then, realising what this might mean, he suddenly looked anxious. 'Where?'

'Right here,' said a voice behind them. It was Molly, also with a mouthful of biscuit and a drink of squash in one hand. 'I've been putting the jigsaw pieces together on the way round – just like Hudson.'

'She's right,' Hudson conceded. 'It's right here, at Macalisters! This is where Mokee Joe hangs out!'

Ash spluttered and nearly choked. Molly slapped him hard on the back.

Hudson stood up. 'Look, you two – can you cover for me? There's somewhere I need to check out. I'll only be a few minutes. If anyone asks, I've just gone to look for the loo!'

'Be careful, Hudson,' Ash warned. 'I don't like the sound of this!'

'Hang on – I'm coming with you!' Molly said firmly.

'No – we can hardly say we've gone off to the loo together! The best thing you can do is cover for me – I'll be back before you know it.'

Molly wasn't happy, but she finally agreed to let him

go on his own, threatening to bring a search party if he wasn't back within ten minutes, and warning that Miss Martin would be most irate if he wasn't back in time.

'Thanks, Molly, thanks, Ash – I'll tell you both the whole story when I get back.'

'I'm not sure I want to know,' Ash said, anxiously looking around in case Miss Martin appeared. 'Anyway, you'd better hurry up. They'll all be out in a minute.'

Hudson crept off towards the Flour Room. His brain was bursting with ideas. He thought back to the day when he'd seen Mokee Joe crawling around on the supermarket floor covered in flour, absorbing it into his body and apparently being recharged by the stuff. If, as it seemed, the creature needed flour to feed on, where better to get it than in a biscuit factory?

And then there was that hole in the fence. It was just big enough for a very thin man – or monster – to crawl through.

Hudson hurried on across the yard. He reached the metal sliding door of the old brick building and opened it just wide enough to squeeze through. There was no-one around, and inside everything was in semi-darkness.

The Flour Room was a dreary, featureless place with a cold unwelcoming atmosphere. Wooden pallets were stacked with bags of flour reaching almost to the ceiling, and everything was covered in white dust.

Hudson edged his way down a narrow passageway between two mountainous rows of flour sacks. He stopped suddenly and looked down at the floor. Fresh footprints had left their impression on the white dust, and they were enormous. They stretched out in front towards the far wall, then disappeared behind one of the huge stacks of bags. Hudson followed them, inching forward cautiously, his heart beating faster as he approached the wall. What if Mokee Joe was waiting around the corner?

It was at this moment that Guardian Angel spoke up.

Follow the footprints if you choose. The Mokee man is not in a fighting mood right now – but take care! The enemy is unpredictable.

So Hudson carried on, and when he reached the wall, he peered round the corner.

Phew! No Mokee Joe. The footprints simply continued on along the wall. His eyes followed them to where they stopped abruptly by another alleyway of flour sacks. But this time he could see a pair of grubby boots sticking out. Someone – or some*thing* – was waiting there, hiding, ready to pounce.

Hudson approached and dared himself to peek round the corner.

Then he had a better idea. He quickly and quietly retraced his steps, sneaking back along the narrow gaps between the pallets and circling around until he came upon the waiting figure from behind.

He had expected to see the back of his enemy, just as he had first seen it in the Castle Supermarket. But to his surprise, all he saw was a pair of empty boots. He sighed with relief and went to take a closer look. Huge and grubby, the boots could only belong to Mokee Joe.

As Hudson knelt and examined them, a firm hand gripped his right shoulder.

Hudson's heart turned to ice. Then a deep voice

bellowed, 'And what do you think you're doing in here, lad?' It was one of the workers, dressed in a pair of white overalls and white cap. Hudson almost threw his arms around the man in gratitude.

'Oh, I'm sorry! I'm with the school party and I got lost!'

'OK, son – but you should be more careful. It's dangerous in a place like this. These sacks are heavy and if one fell on you . . . Well, it doesn't bear thinking about.'

Hudson followed the man back towards the sliding door, and was directed across the yard to where Ash was still waiting patiently on the bench. The other children were coming out of the reception and lining up to board the coach. Molly was at the front of the line, looking around anxiously. The factory worker walked off, leaving Hudson hovering in the doorway for a moment.

Just as he was about to leave, he felt a sudden compulsion to look back again. And there, high above the empty boots, was the long, reclining form of his enemy. The creature was lying quite still on its side, on top of a mountain of flour sacks, its head supported by one spindly elbow. The blue glow was so bright it was almost purple. And though the fiend's face was hidden between its hat and collar, Hudson felt certain it was sneering at him. But this time, he was determined to show he wasn't frightened, and stared back in defiance.

And so the two enemies glared at each other, weighing each other up, trying to read each other's thoughts . . . The situation reminded Hudson of a gunfight in a cowboy film. But instead of guns, this was a battle of minds, each resolved to outwit the other.

A voice from outside broke the spell. 'Hudson Brown,

get over here this instant!' It was Miss Martin.

Hudson took one last look at his enemy and prepared to leave, but as he turned, something struck him between the shoulder blades. He wheeled round, but now there was no-one there, only a small bag of flour lying burst at his feet.

Something was written on it. He quickly picked up the bag, tore off the paper with the writing on it and put it in his pocket. Then he sprinted back across the yard. By this time the children were already on the coach and Miss Martin, who had just completed her seventeenth head count of the day, did not look happy.

'Where on Earth have you been? And look at the state of you! Your back's covered in flour. Hudson – I really expected better of you!'

Molly grinned at him with her 'Don't say I didn't warn you' grin. Hudson apologised and climbed meekly aboard.

On the return journey, he told Molly and Ash all about the incident in the Flour Room. Taking the creased piece of paper from his pocket, he read the scrawled message aloud.

'Guardian Angel have I none, Hudson Brown is my maker's son,

Sixth day coming, sixth day night, I'll kill that boy in the pale moonlight!

MJ'

The first line was too cryptic for anyone to solve. But Ash, who was good at puzzles, quickly worked out the meaning of the second line. He looked at Hudson, his face as white as a sheet and his bottom lip beginning to tremble.

'Hudson, I don't know how to tell you this . . . Mokee Joe is coming to get you – to kill you – on *Saturday night*!'

9

Neighbourhood Watch

Next day, as Hudson and Molly walked up the towpath towards the junction with Kiln Street, Hudson was still reeling from the shock of Mokee Joe's message. Why would anyone or anything possibly want to kill *him*? What had *he* ever done to hurt anybody? Maybe this was still a horrible nightmare and he would wake up at any moment. After all, life was becoming more and more of a clash between dreams and reality, and it was getting increasingly difficult to tell them apart.

Molly tugged at his sleeve, reminding him that this was indeed reality. She pointed in the direction of the iron bridge and as they approached the spot where Ash had lost his fishing tackle, memories of the previous Sunday came flooding back.

'Hudson – over there on the far bank. Doesn't it make your flesh crawl?'

Hudson looked across and saw the charred frame of Ash's umbrella, a testament to the bizarre events that had recently taken place there. At the sight of it, the two friends instinctively looked up at the bridge again, hoping not to see what they were afraid they might see.

'Come on. Let's go down Kiln Street and see if we can find number 13,' Hudson said.

Molly grabbed him by the arm. 'What are we waiting for?'

Hudson could see by her face that she meant business.

Kiln Street was a slum: two rows of run-down terraced houses and in between, piles of rubble, old tin cans, discarded chip cartons and pieces of rusted metal littering the cobbled road. As Ash had said, most of the houses were empty and boarded up, but a few had dingy curtains at the windows, indicating that people might still be living there. Yet there was no sign of life, which added to the street's forbidding atmosphere. As the two friends walked further up the road, they began to feel very out of place.

'I don't like it here, Hudson,' Molly commented. 'I mean, who would live in a place like this?'

'Dodgy people, like Ash said,' Hudson replied, looking around with distaste at the squalor. 'Or maybe just people who are desperate,' he added, suddenly thinking of his own nice home and disliking himself for being so prejudiced.

It did not take them long to find number 13. This

house looked even more run-down than the rest. The two upstairs windows and one downstairs were cracked and covered in grime, their insides lined with old newspapers, though the lower window also had a pair of faded lace curtains. Most of the paint had been chipped from the battered door and the house number looked as if it had been painted on by a none too steady hand. Someone had scrawled 'Weirdo' in black paint across the bottom. It was hard to believe that anyone lived inside.

Suddenly, a door behind them opened and a throaty voice called out: 'What do you think you're up to, creeping about outside my door?'

Hudson and Molly spun round to see a short, scrunched-up old woman eyeing them with a mistrustful look.

'Sorry,' Molly answered. 'We didn't mean to disturb you. We were just looking for number 13.'

The woman looked even more suspicious. She folded her arms across her chest and continued to stare. Hudson noticed that she seemed particularly fascinated by his hairstyle; then she began giving Molly the once-over.

'And what would you be wanting with number 13?' she demanded.

'Well, I think that's our business, if you don't mind,' Molly replied indignantly, folding her own arms in a deliberate mockery of the woman's pose.

Hudson looked at his friend with approval, then back to the old woman to see her response. She was adjusting her headscarf and poking at some curlers showing through at the front.

'Whoever's business it is, you'll be lucky if anybody answers *that* door. Nobody round here has ever seen who lives there. Complete crank, if you ask me!'

Hudson had to stop himself from saying that no-one *was* asking her, and that it took a crank to know one, but he didn't want to cause any trouble or attract attention. So he simply asked, 'If nobody ever sees who lives in there, how do you know the house isn't empty?'

'Ah, you may well ask.' The old woman folded her arms again. 'There's milk delivered every day and sometimes the odd box of groceries left on the doorstep and they're always taken in. But I've still never managed to see anyone. It's enough to give you the creeps!' She scowled. 'Anyway, I haven't got all day to stand here gossiping. I've got my telly to watch. I'll leave you to it – but I wouldn't hold my breath if I were you.' And saying this she turned, walked back into her own house and slammed the door.

Hudson and Molly giggled. A curtain twitched as the old woman continued watching from inside.

'Come on, Hudson, let's give it a try and get this over with,' Molly said.

Hudson marched up to the door of number 13, taking care not to trip over the rubble. He banged on the rotting wood as hard as he could.

There was no reply.

'Hudson, look!'

Molly was pointing and Hudson's heart sank as he saw why. A police car was slowly cruising along Kiln Street in their direction.

'I think we need to make ourselves scarce, Molly.

They'll want to know what we're doing here and start asking all sorts of questions.'

'Right,' she agreed, 'let's get out of here. We can hide in the brickworks again, on the corner.'

They dashed back towards the towpath and headed for the old factory. After hiding in the shadows for a few minutes, they watched in silence as the police car pulled up right outside. Hudson nudged Molly as two policemen got out and started walking towards the canal.

'Oh no – it's the same policemen that came to school,' he sighed. 'Look, that's the one who talked to us with Fletcher.'

'Mmm, you're right,' Molly frowned. 'D'you think they're looking for us?'

'Could be. I bet that nosy old woman phoned the police. If they find us, we're in trouble! Just keep down.'

They lay low and waited. After five minutes the policemen returned to the car and they could hear the sergeant's voice clearly.

'Well, at least there's no sign of him tonight.'

'No, and I can't say I'm sorry,' the other policeman answered. 'Sounds like a real nasty piece of work to me. How many reports have we had now?'

'Eight!' the sergeant answered grimly, 'and always kids. It seems he's got it in for 'em.'

Hudson and Molly began to shiver in their damp hiding place – and not just with the cold.

'That poor lad from Carlisle Street was fished out of the canal with a broken arm. He was lucky he didn't drown.'

'How could someone do that to a kid? Snivelling coward! Why doesn't he pick on someone his own size?'

'Actually, it's not always kids and it's not a question of being a coward,' the sergeant went on in a serious voice. 'You should have seen what he did to those three men in Tennyson Road. I know one of them – Jack Hoskins – a real tough case. He doesn't look too pretty now!'

Hudson and Molly shivered again as two car doors slammed, followed by the sound of an engine roaring away.

Molly breathed more deeply. 'Thank God they've gone.'

'And I think we should do the same,' Hudson added. Warning bells were already ringing in his head. He stood up, paced about and began to adjust his watch.

'OK, Hudson, spit it out – what are you thinking?'

He didn't answer at first, just stood absolutely still with his eyes closed.

'Hudson – what *is* it?'

'GA's coming through loud and clear. We've got to get away from here right now – and *fast*!'

He almost dragged Molly to the doorway of the factory. At first they thought the coast was clear, but then Molly spotted something.

'Hudson! Look! On the bridge!'

Hudson followed her gaze and gasped. Like a horrible case of déjà vu, the towering figure was staring menacingly from the middle of the bridge. But then Mokee Joe began to scuttle, spider-like, down the steps and onto the towpath. He had never looked so predatory.

'I'm just going to have to face him,' Hudson said bravely. 'I know I've got to sooner or later and with GA helping me . . .'

'No, Hudson! Not this time. Hang on a sec.' Molly bit her lip. 'I've got a plan that just might work and give that creep a shock. I've seen this done in a film . . .'

But as Molly began to explain, Hudson interrupted her. 'You can't do that on your own!' he protested. 'It's suicide!'

Molly ignored him and quickly finished telling him her plan while she removed her denim jacket and handed it to him. As heavy footsteps sounded nearer and nearer, they both looked up the towpath and Hudson realised there was no more time for discussion. Mokee Joe was closing in on them.

Hudson thought of the hideous face of his nightmares.

'OK, Molly – go for it!' He squeezed her hand and then sprinted off down the towpath.

Molly dived back into the doorway. She crouched down and prepared herself.

Hudson ran on. He knew that at this moment, the monster was only interested in him, not Molly – which was why, he hoped, her plan might just work. Even so, her timing had to be spot on. She would only have one chance.

A few seconds later, still running, he turned and looked over his shoulder. He was just in time to see Mokee Joe reach the doorway of the brickworks, and Molly dive out to grab the creature's feet.

Hudson grimaced as it crashed headfirst over her and crunched into the gravel. It hit the ground with such force that it skidded along for at least another ten metres before smashing into a pile of bricks, where it lay quite still. Molly, meanwhile, picked herself up and ran to join Hudson, deliberately trampling over the wide-brimmed black hat as she went. Hudson watched her with admiration.

'Yes, Molly – you did it!' he whooped. He wanted to hug her, but they sprinted on and never stopped running until they were almost home.

Outside Molly's gate, Hudson hugged her at last.

'Molly, you're the cleverest, bravest best friend anyone could ever want, and I'd never have believed anyone could . . .' He went on and on.

Molly smiled and blushed, finally cutting him short. 'Thanks,' she said, 'but I've really got to go. I don't want to miss my Judo class. We girls have to learn how to protect ourselves, you know!' And she took her denim jacket from him and walked up the path to her house, whistling as if nothing extraordinary had happened.

Hudson watched her go and laughed for the first time in ages.

Sauntering up Tennyson Road towards number 13, Hudson thought that at least tonight he could relax. Surely it would be quite a while before his enemy recovered from that spectacular fall?

He walked in the front door and was greeted by the smell of cooking. He'd never felt so hungry!

'Hudson is that you?' a voice called from the kitchen.

'Yes, Mum. Sorry I'm a bit late. Had to go somewhere with Molly.'

'Oh, that's OK. Your dad's only just finished in the garden so the tea's a bit late anyway.'

Hudson dumped his faded leather flying jacket on the bottom stair and went straight upstairs to wash his hands. As he was drying them, he suddenly felt drawn over to the bath. He looked down and saw the biggest spider he'd ever seen crawling about in the bottom. Spiders had always fascinated him, but for some reason this huge one seemed special and he knew what he had to do. He went downstairs to fetch an empty matchbox.

'Spiffy,' he whispered as he placed it gently inside. 'I'll call you Spiffy. You and me are going to be good friends and in some way I can sense that you're going to be a big help to me.' He took the matchbox, scrawled a big cross on it and placed it on his dressing table before going downstairs for his tea.

'Did you have a good day at Macalisters, son?' his mother asked, putting a steaming plate of homemade lasagne in front of him.

Hudson wondered what she would have said if he told her all that had really happened. 'Yeah, it was a great day and we got to try lots of biscuits.'

'But did you learn anything?' Mr Brown joined in as he came in from the garden.

'Oh yes, Dad. I certainly learnt a thing or two,' Hudson replied mysteriously.

Mrs Brown sat down and poured out the tea. 'Before I forget, there was a parcel waiting for you on the doorstep. No stamp or anything, but it's got your name on it.'

Hudson tensed. And then a feeling of warmth came over him as he sensed the parcel held no danger. 'It's probably something from Ash,' he said matter-of-factly.

But his tea went down a little more quickly than usual and before long, Hudson was in the privacy of his bedroom, opening the small package. He hadn't a clue what it was. He was even more puzzled when he found a CD inside, entitled '*Spirit of the East – Music for Meditation*'.

A note attached to it read: '*Play track 7 into your ears only and tonight we shall finally meet.*'

Now what does all this mean? Hudson pondered. He wished that Ash was there to help him understand the message. Oh yes! Suddenly he remembered that he'd promised to e-mail Ash.

'Think I'll phone him instead and ask him about this now,' he said to himself.

A few minutes later, he and Ash were deep in conversation. As Hudson went over what had happened at the brickworks, including Molly's heroic deed, Ash could only react with 'Wow!', 'Wicked!', 'Great!' and 'Unbelievable!'

'Oh, and by the way, Ash,' Hudson finally chipped in, 'I've just got a package with a CD in it and the message '*Play into your ears only*'. What d'you think that means?'

'Simple, Hudson,' Ash replied without hesitation. 'Play it on your headphones.'

Ash made it sound so obvious, Hudson felt rather foolish.

'Thanks, Ash. And don't forget to keep Saturday night free – if you're sure you're up for it.'

Ash said he wasn't really sure he was 'up for it', but he would make a point of being there because he thought that Hudson might need all the help he could get. And then he rang off.

Hudson went upstairs. What with all the recent perplexing events, he felt absolutely exhausted. Once in his room, he hardly dared look down from the window towards the dreaded spot. But he did and, much to his relief, there were no lurking shadows.

After undressing, he climbed into bed and closed his eyes. Then he remembered the CD. He took the disc from its package and placed it in his personal CD player, put on the headphones and thought about the strange message again – especially the words '*tonight we shall meet*'.

Feeling a little nervous, he lay back and pressed the PLAY button.

10

Riding High

Hudson's ears filled with the sounds of traditional Indian music. The enchanting echoes of the *sitar* and the *shehnai* penetrated deep into his mind and his bath-time training with Guardian Angel allowed him to rise up easily, leaving his sleeping body below.

The soothing spiritual music accompanied him as he floated upwards to the bedroom ceiling and then his body flipped over, just as it had done that time in the bathroom. But this time there was no panic about getting back. Hudson just tuned himself in more deeply to the bewitching sounds and allowed his body to pass through into the attic and then still further up, through the roof.

He felt so relaxed and at peace with himself as he

drifted out into the starry night and found himself looking down at rows and rows of red roof tiles. He could see Pugwash sat by the chimney, like a sentry on guard, and he called out to him. But there was no response; it seemed his floating 'other self' was completely invisible, even to his furry friend.

Drifting over the narrow opening between his house and next door's, Hudson looked down and saw that the familiar crouching shape was back, lurking between the dustbins. But this time it didn't worry him. He felt completely in command of the situation.

Hovering a little lower, he got a clear view of the top of Mokee Joe's hat and the dirty grey raincoat trailing out beneath it. Hudson suddenly realised that here was an opportunity to attack his unsuspecting enemy from above. So he reached out and tried to pick up a heavy roof tile that had slipped into the guttering. But this was not his physical self and his hands simply passed through it like a phantom passing through a wall.

Reluctantly, he left the skulking 'rat' below and floated high above the roofs towards his true destination.

And still the Indian music filled his ears.

As he moved on, he traced his route along the familiar streets far below – down Tennyson Road, left along Byron Road and on past Molly's house. He was really tempted to drop in through her roof and check what she was up to, but now the force was pulling him too strongly.

A few minutes later the black, inky water of the Danvers and Dearne Canal materialised below. He could just make out the towpath and he followed its course out of Danvers Green and up towards the old brickworks.

He was almost there.

Finally, dropping slowly downwards towards Kiln Street, Hudson was surprised to see the tops of a small group of heads standing outside number 13. The crowd looked agitated and one man was banging on the door. Another was throwing stones at the windows.

He floated up to the roof of the dilapidated house and allowed himself to pass through it to the inside. This was the moment he'd been eagerly anticipating. For he knew who was waiting for him there.

If the outside of the house was run-down, the inside was even worse.

On the upstairs landing, Hudson looked around. The wallpaper was peeling off and the floorboards were dirty and uncarpeted. He passed through a wall into a dingy, damp bedroom littered with piles of papers and dusty books, and he knew he was now directly above the room where he needed to be. He passed through the floor so that he was looking down from the ceiling to the room below.

Unlike the rest of the house, this room was tidy. In fact, it was almost cosy.

There was only one chair – a single armchair – and from above Hudson could see the bald head of the person sitting in it, their arms stretched out along the arms of the chair. A voice he knew well called out to him.

'Welcome, Hudson. I've been expecting you.'

Hudson drifted down until he was directly opposite the seated figure. Its physical appearance gave him quite a shock, but mentally he knew he was in good company.

It looked like a man, but the bald head was bigger than any Hudson had ever seen and seemed to be divided into four distinct lobes. Hudson immediately thought of his own hairstyle. The slightly protruding eyes were all white, the pupils rolled back in a trance-like state, and he recognised it as the same face he'd seen in the mirror in Candleshed.

The figure was dressed in a threadbare white shirt, collarless and full of creases. A pair of plain black trousers, odd socks and tatty carpet slippers completed the outfit. It was obvious that this being was not too concerned with its outward appearance.

Hudson stared, thinking that it looked distinctly alien.

'You know who I am, don't you?'

'Yes,' Hudson replied without hesitation. 'You're Guardian Angel!'

'In your Earth language, I suppose that's true. In fact my real name is Dek-3-ergon.'

'Well, it's great to meet you face to face at last,' Hudson continued politely. 'As you know, my name's Hudson.'

'That may well be your Earth name but your real name is Tor-3-ergon. In Earth terms, you are my nephew.'

This information shocked Hudson and he wanted to know more. 'If you're my uncle, tell me – where are we from?'

'Alcatron-3. That is why we have a "3" in our name. Alcatron-3 is the third planet in the Plexus System, the system with a bright orange sun at its centre.'

'Betelgeuse,' Hudson said knowingly. 'I thought so. Whenever I look towards the constellation of Orion, I'm drawn to that star and I start feeling homesick.'

'These are all Earth terms,' the figure continued. '*We* know the orange sun as the Plexus star – a bright unstable star and one that will eventually collapse in on itself, but not for another twenty billion Earth years.'

'Who are my true parents?' Hudson suddenly asked. 'And why are we here, and—?'

'One question at a time,' Guardian Angel interrupted in a calm voice. 'You can only absorb so much data at once.'

Hudson was so engrossed listening to Guardian Angel that he was at first only dimly aware of the loud banging on the door of the house, and the shouting outside.

'Your father was Hud-3-ergon, my twin. We were both born with enlarged heads, increased intelligence and telepathic powers. Some say we represent the next stage of evolution of the Alcatron people. Your father became a brilliant scientist and an expert in cybernetics. He was also extremely unhappy and often depressed.'

'But why – if he was such a clever scientist?' Hudson demanded.

'Unfortunately, because of our strange appearance, we were both bullied mercilessly throughout our childhood and consequently your father bore a grudge against society – and especially children – for the rest of his life. He only had one true love – your mother.'

'Does my mother live on Alcatron-3?' Hudson asked, getting very excited now.

Guardian Angel hesitated before answering. 'Your mother is dead. She died giving birth to you.'

Hudson gulped and took a few moments to absorb this before asking: 'And my father?'

'I'm afraid he is dead too.'

Hudson sensed the emotion in Guardian Angel's mental voice and the sharing of his own sorrow.

'How did he die?'

'As I've said, he was a very bitter man. He hated children and then you came along and inadvertently caused the death of his wife.'

'So then he hated me as well?' Hudson asked sadly.

'I'm afraid that's true. His hatred caused him to go insane and he finally decided to exact his revenge.'

'On me?'

'Yes, on you,' Guardian Angel went on. 'And also on all children. He put an evil plan into operation and then took his own life.'

Hudson had barely started his next question before Guardian Angel spoke again. 'You doubtless want to know about the Mokee Joe creature?'

'Yes. Who is he? Or should I say what is it?'

The banging on the door grew louder.

'I have little time to answer. Let me just say that your father is responsible for the monstrosity that is programmed to terrorise children and to destroy you, and it will not rest until it is successful.'

'But why here, billions of miles away from Alcatron 3?'

'Back on our own planet, the creature caused havoc, as you can imagine. Fortunately, before it got to you it was cornered by security forces and took refuge in a space pod. It was a simple task . . .'

'. . . to blast it into deep space,' Hudson concluded.

'Exactly. But at the time, no-one could have predicted that the creature would finish up on a planet inhabited by life-forms similar to our own.'

'And a planet with so many children,' Hudson added.

'Correct again, Tor-3-Ergon. And now you and I are here to lure the demon out and rid this planet of its evil existence. You are its prime target – you draw it like a magnet.'

Hudson looked at Guardian Angel with soulful eyes. 'Mmm, I've noticed. It seems to know more and more where I am and what I'm up to.'

Guardian Angel continued with sympathy in his voice: 'Like us, it has telepathic abilities and it can impress its mind on its subjects. This is why it waits outside your dwelling during the hours of darkness.'

'So is that why I keep having nightmares, because Mokee Joe forces himself into my head?' Hudson asked incredulously.

'Exactly right,' Guardian Angel confirmed. 'The boundary between dreams and reality is indeed a thin one.'

'You're telling me!' Hudson agreed, thinking about his bruised wrist.

The banging was getting louder still and Hudson noted Guardian Angel was now communicating more quickly.

'As you know, Mokee Joe is coming to challenge you on Saturday evening.'

'Yes, I got a message—'

'I know of his threat,' Guardian Angel interrupted. 'Rest assured that I shall be there to help you but you will also need the help of another friend.'

'Oh, you mean Molly?' Hudson offered.

'Molly and Ash are of course valuable companions, but I speak of an eight-legged friend—'

But Guardian Angel never finished. The door to the little sitting-room almost broke off its rusty hinges as two policemen, followed by a small group of onlookers, smashed their way in.

Hudson put his arms up to protect himself, but no-one seemed to notice he was there. And then he realised he *wasn't* there. Not in body, anyway.

He floated back up towards the ceiling and watched helplessly as Guardian Angel was lifted out of the chair and handcuffed. He recognised the unpleasant old woman from the house opposite standing in the background, arms folded.

'About time too!' she was squawking. 'There'll be no more attacks on children now. The sooner that brute's safely behind bars, the better!'

'Weirdo – pervert!' the others in the group shouted as Guardian Angel was led away.

Hudson received his final message just as the police car pulled away.

'Don't worry,' Guardian Angel reassured him. 'They think that I am responsible for the attacks by the Educator. They'll take me to the police station, but I will still be able to keep in communication with you from there. Remember – together we can destroy him. But we must never underestimate his powers.'

Hudson floated back to the rooftops, his mind reeling.

He called him the Educator. That must surely be the second 'E' in MOKEE. Ministry Of Kinetics – Electronic Educator.

But before he could give the matter any more thought, he became aware that the mystic music, which had been in his subconscious throughout his trip, was now beginning to fade. He began to feel a pulling sensation, just like the one he had felt when Mr Brown had applied the cold flannel to his head.

And then the music stopped completely and the force propelling him increased dramatically. Hudson suddenly found himself flying homeward at high speed over the rooftops, like Superman. Soon he could see his house far below, but to his horror he kept on going. *He couldn't stop.*

On and on he soared, towards the centre of Danvers Green.

'Oh please! *Somebody help me!*' he shouted into the night. But he knew it was useless. This wasn't his physical self. No-one could see or hear him.

And then, just as real panic began to set in, he felt himself starting to fall. A large familiar building loomed below and Hudson could see that he was descending rapidly towards it. The force pulling him down grew stronger and stronger until he was sure he was going to smash into the ground.

Down, down he went, ever faster.

And then he woke up.

With blurry eyes, he looked at the familiar faces around his bed and then to the doctor writing on a clipboard.

'Well, Hudson, you've done it again,' his father said with a deep frown. 'You've frightened the living daylights out of us!'

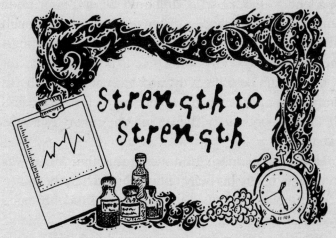

11

Strength to Strength

Hudson sat bolt upright in his bed. 'Where am I?'

Mrs Brown took hold of his hand. 'Oh, Hudson! We've been so worried about you!'

'But I've never felt so good,' he said, looking around the room in bewilderment. 'Will somebody please tell me where I am?'

'You're in Danvers Green Hospital and you've been asleep since Tuesday.' The doctor spoke without bothering to look up from his clipboard.

Hudson stretched and yawned. 'What day is it now?'

'Friday.' The doctor still didn't look up.

Hudson was shocked. '*Whoahh* . . . hang on a minute! You mean . . .?'

'Yes, son!' Mr Brown said sombrely. 'You've been

asleep for three days and three nights!'

The doctor finally put down the clipboard and took hold of Hudson's wrist.

'You're a puzzle, young man, you really are. When your parents brought you in here, your heart rate had dropped to half of what it should be and your body temperature had dropped by ten degrees. That's enough to kill a normal person. You're quite a celebrity amongst the staff here now!' Hudson started to fidget as the doctor continued to hold his wrist and look at his watch. 'In fact we'd quite like it if you could stay on for a few days,' the doctor continued. 'There's still one or two tests we'd like to do.'

Hudson couldn't help noticing that the doctor was looking at where his belly button should have been.

And then the words 'Saturday night' suddenly came into Hudson's mind.

'What day did you say it was?' he asked again.

'It's Friday,' the doctor said.

Hudson looked back towards Mrs Brown. 'I want to go home! I feel fine!'

'That's for the doctor to decide,' Mrs Brown answered. 'You're looking well enough now, I admit, but we want to be sure that everything is as it should be.'

Hudson looked back to the doctor, who was frowning and didn't look too pleased at Hudson's suggestion. He put his hands in the pockets of his white coat and turned towards Mrs Brown. 'He may still be a little weak. I really think it might be better for us to keep him for at least another twenty-four hours.'

Hudson did not like the sound of this idea at all. He was feeling wide-awake and full of energy. In fact, he felt strangely recharged and extremely strong. He needed to get back home, back to Molly and Ash, ready for the following night – *the* night. He stared at the doctor with a determined expression.

'I suppose I'll just have to show you how well I feel.'

Before anyone could say anything, he had leapt out of the bed and walked towards the corner of the room. A metal trolley with two shelves stood there, the lower shelf filled with books and the top shelf holding a large TV set.

'What are you doing?' the doctor asked angrily.

Without a word, Hudson reached down and gripped one of the metal legs close to the floor. With one hand, he lifted the trolley – books, TV and all – up into the air. He stood there proudly, holding the enormous weight high above his head.

There were gasps from his audience and especially from the doctor.

'OK, lad,' Mr Brown said, looking half-shocked and half-proud, 'get your clothes on – you're going home.' He looked at his wife. 'Well, he certainly looks fit enough to me!'

After this demonstration, Hudson sensed that the doctor was even keener to detain him for more tests; but no-one could dispute that he'd got his strength back, and so reluctantly it was agreed that he could be discharged.

One hour later, all three Browns were back in 13, Tennyson Road. It was twelve noon.

Hudson tucked into his second helping of sausages, chips and beans.

'Where's he putting it all?' Mr Brown said in

astonishment. 'That's what I want to know.'

'It's hardly surprising,' Mrs Brown answered, passing over some more bread and butter. 'His body's been without food for three days.'

The way Mr and Mrs Brown were talking about him as if he wasn't there made Hudson wonder if he really was. But the food tasted good – it was definitely real.

Hudson emptied his plate for the second time and looked up expectantly. 'Mum, could I have one more sausage and another spoonful of beans, please?'

'It's like watching a human waste-disposal machine!' Mr Brown observed with a hint of reproach. He stood up. 'I'm away into the garden before the rain sets in.'

Mrs Brown spooned more beans onto Hudson's plate. She sat opposite as he began his third helping. He could see the concern in her eyes.

'Hudson, this is all so strange. Can you just tell me – is everything all right?'

'Sort of!' Hudson replied with his mouth half full. 'Mum, do you know where I'm from?'

'What do you mean?' Mrs Brown asked with a slightly uncomfortable edge to her voice.

'Well, I know that you and Dad aren't my real parents and we both know about my little "differences". And now this deep sleep and the way I've woken up feeling super strong. It's all a bit unreal, you have to admit!'

Mrs Brown smiled and hesitated. Then she took a deep breath. 'Well, the truth is that your background *is* a mystery. We don't really know how you came to be on our doorstep when you did, but we had no problem about taking you in and we've never regretted it. You've been a joy to us, Hudson.'

He cut off another piece of sausage and put it in his mouth. He could see that tears were forming in his mum's eyes and he wasn't sure what to say next. He chewed thoughtfully and then continued.

'There's been all sorts of things going on lately, Mum, and I want you to know that whatever happens, I'll always think of you and Dad as my real parents.'

'Bless you, son,' she said. 'Of course me and your dad know that you're different, but you're different in a nice way and you'll always be our Hudson.'

Hudson was moved. He thought how very special Mr and Mrs Brown were to him. He couldn't imagine them not being there.

'Just remember,' Mrs Brown went on as she poured him a cup of steaming tea, 'me and your dad will always be here for you.'

Feeling reassured by their chat, Hudson began to think about his stomach again. He looked up at his mum with a smile.

'What's for pudding, Mum – and will there be seconds?'

Hudson was striding towards Danvers Green Primary School. He had talked his mum into allowing him to meet Molly and Ash at the school gates. At first, she'd not been keen on the idea but she'd finally relented on the condition that he came straight back home afterwards.

It was just five minutes before the end of class as Hudson walked up to the playground railings. He peered into his classroom and could see his empty place by the window. He could also make out Mr Trueman writing on the board.

Grabbing hold of the railings, he stood on tiptoe and strained to see further into the classroom. He quickly picked out the familiar figure of Molly, who had already seen him and was waving. He waved back. Soon the rest of 6T had noticed him too. In fact, before long, it seemed that everyone in the class was aware of him – everyone except old Trueman, who was still scribbling away.

Hudson decided to show off. He walked up to the two railings forced apart by his enemy a few days earlier. As Molly and the rest of the class watched, he squeezed the thick iron bars with all his strength. He could feel the power flowing from his muscles into the metal and even he had to gasp as they bent back to their original position.

Eat your heart out, Mokee Joe, he thought to himself, just as the bell sounded for the end of school.

Molly was first through the school gates. 'Hudson! You're OK! What happened?' She ran up to him and Hudson just managed to restrain himself from throwing his arms around her.

'It's a long story,' he said, smiling. 'I'll tell you later. The main thing is, I feel fine. In fact, I've never felt better!'

'I think we've all seen that!' Molly said excitedly. 'How did you do that bar bending trick?'

'No trick – just brute strength. Something amazing happened to my body while I was asleep.'

'You mean you were only *asleep*?' Hudson watched her big brown eyes open wide. 'Everyone was so worried, Hudson. Did your mum tell you – I came to the hospital three times but you were always . . . Well, I thought you were in some sort of coma.'

'I know,' he said, trying to sound grateful. 'It's all been really weird. Honest, I will explain later, but right now I can only think about Saturday.'

'You're telling me!' Molly replied. 'It's all me and Ash have been thinking about as well. But I was beginning to wonder whether you'd be back with us in time.'

Hudson looked over Molly's shoulder as a stream of pupils started filing out of the gate. 'Here's Ash.'

Ash, wearing a big grin, walked up and joined them. 'Hey, Hudson! Great to have you back again. You really had us worried this time.'

Hudson listened while Molly and Ash gave him all the school gossip – and then it was his turn.

As they walked home, chatting excitedly, Hudson felt so good to be back. With his new strength, his friends around him and Guardian Angel tuning in, he suddenly felt he could face anything – even Saturday night.

Tomorrow, Mokee Joe would be dead meat.

Saturday finally arrived.

Hudson, Molly and Ash headed down the garden towards Candleshed, all with butterflies fluttering wildly in their stomachs. Hudson carried half a dozen new red candles and two matchboxes, one marked with a cross. Molly brought the snacks and Ash struggled with a huge CD player to supply the music. It would, he claimed, keep their minds off their worries.

As they made their way to their meeting place, Hudson could see that his father was working on his beloved vegetable patch.

'Hello there! Looks like it's going to be a long meeting,' Mr Brown called out, leaning on his spade. 'I don't suppose we'll be seeing you lot until after dark!'

Once inside Candleshed, they laid everything out on the old wooden table. Hudson was pleased to see Ash produce a mobile phone.

'This could come in really useful if we're under attack!' Ash said. 'I persuaded Dad to lend it to me in case I needed a lift home – but he said not to throw it in any canals if I can help it!'

'Brilliant!' Hudson and Molly said together. Whether or not it offered any real security, having the phone would definitely make them feel better.

'OK,' Hudson said, rubbing his hands together. 'Let's set some booby traps.'

'Wicked!' Ash said. 'But you'll have to show me how.'

Hudson looked at Molly. 'Do you want to help?'

But Molly was already reclining in one of the old armchairs, engrossed in a book. 'No, I'll look after things in here, if you don't mind.'

'What's that you're reading?' Hudson enquired.

She held up the cover of the book. 'It's a book on Judo. Our instructor recommended it. I'm doing some last-minute revision on some moves.'

'OK – carry on!' Hudson said. 'That could come in very useful again before long. Come on, Ash – let's go.'

Outside the door, Hudson looked up the garden and saw that Mr Brown was still busy. He was digging a deep trench alongside the runner bean plants and seemed far too preoccupied to question what the boys were up to.

They tied lengths of string between pegs set into the ground and attached empty tin cans, so that if anyone tripped over the string, the noise would raise the alarm. They also dug a few deep holes and covered them with bits of old wood and grass cuttings.

By four o'clock, the Candleshed defences were ready.

'Well, that should do it,' Hudson said. 'The shed's got traps all the way round it.'

'And there's plenty of alarms set along the fence,' Ash added, wiping his forehead with his sleeve.

Hudson noted that Mr Brown had finished his trench and gone indoors – probably to catch up with the football results.

'OK, let's get back inside and see what Molly's up to.'

'Sure thing,' Ash agreed. 'In any case, it's starting to get dark and I don't feel so safe out here any more.'

But before they went in, Hudson climbed on top of the compost heap in the bottom corner of the garden. He took one last look around, then he and Ash returned to base.

By 5.30pm, it was almost dark. Hudson, Molly and Ash sat picking at sweets and sipping at drinks. Pop tunes rang out from the CD player and Ash hummed along with his mouth full – anything to keep their minds off the horror outside.

'I think we should turn the radio off,' Hudson said suddenly.

'Why?' Ash asked, sounding disappointed. 'The music helps me to stay calm.'

Molly reached over and switched it off. 'So that we can hear the enemy approaching,' she said firmly. 'You're a real dork at times, Ash.' She and Hudson exchanged a knowing glance.

'Exactly right,' Hudson agreed. 'We need to have all our senses on full alert.'

Now the shed seemed very quiet. All around, candles flickered, casting dancing shadows on the walls.

Hudson checked his watch. 'It won't be long now.'

He looked at Ash's face and noticed tiny beads of sweat forming on his forehead. 'Try to keep calm. Together, we can do this.'

Molly was looking into the dusty glass mirror, fiddling with her hair. Hudson wondered if it really needed fixing, or whether she was just trying to keep busy.

As the evening closed in and darkness invaded the garden, everyone felt the atmosphere in Candleshed grow more and more tense. They all strained their ears for the slightest sound. A faint rumble of thunder echoed in the distance.

'This is getting more and more like a horror film,' Molly commented, chewing a strand of hair that had come loose.

'Except this is real,' Hudson reminded her.

Ash almost jumped out of his skin as his mobile emitted two loud beeps. 'It'll be my dad,' he said, picking up the phone. 'Probably checking to see what time I need a lift home.'

But then Hudson watched as Ash's face changed – he had stopped smiling and was looking puzzled.

'I've just realised, it's a text,' he said. 'But no-one ever sends texts on Dad's phone!'

'What does it say?' Molly asked impatiently.

Ash pressed the keys to bring the message up on the display and his eyes grew wider with every new word that appeared.

'What's up?' Hudson asked anxiously.

'What's it say?' Molly asked nervously.

A stunned Ash passed the phone over to Hudson. 'Here – you read it,' he said.

By now, Hudson had guessed who the message was from. He read it out slowly:

'Don't-go-out-or-up-to-bed . . . am-on-my-way-to-Candleshed . . . MJ-is-coming!'

At 6.30pm all was still quiet. No-one was speaking.

Hudson and his two friends sat utterly still and strained even harder to hear any sounds that might indicate the approach of the enemy; but all was silent.

Hudson smiled wanly at Molly. She was wearing a zip-up leather jacket with a bright silver star on the breast pocket, and looked calm and determined.

She smiled back at him and whispered, 'Which way will he come?'

'I've been thinking about that,' Hudson whispered back. 'I'm sure he won't come past the house and I can't imagine he would climb over the stone wall at the bottom of the garden – it's too high.'

'Well, what other way is there?' Molly asked, her face glowing in the candlelight.

Hudson turned to Ash with a questioning look.

'I think he'll sneak down one of the neighbours' gardens and then climb over the fence,' Ash suggested.

Neither of Candleshed's two windows faced the neighbours' fences and Ash's theory made them feel even more vulnerable.

Molly echoed everybody's thoughts. 'So we won't see him coming.'

'No – but we'll hear him,' Hudson reassured her. 'Don't forget, we've set the alarms.'

Hudson started fiddling with his watch as an eerie silence descended again on the shed.

After another very long minute, Hudson came up with a plan.

'Look – Molly – you take one window and I'll take the other.' He stood up and put his hands in his pockets. 'Ash – you keep guard over by the door.'

'What do you mean by "keep guard"?' Ash asked timidly.

'Just open the door slightly and peer out towards the fence. Let us know if you see anything suspicious. Molly and me – we'll be watching up and down the garden.'

They each went to their stations and the nerve-racking wait went on. The candles burnt lower. The darkness closed in and the shadows lengthened. Hudson couldn't help noticing that his own shadow looked particularly menacing.

'Sshhh . . . !' Hudson suddenly whispered, tilting his head back. 'I think I can hear something.' He stared up at the roof.

They all looked up and listened. Sure enough, a footfall sounded above their heads followed a few seconds later by another, then another.

Hudson watched as Molly and Ash's faces turned sickly white. Like him, they could imagine only too well what was moving about above them. But how could he have got up there?

'Do you think it's really him?' Molly asked quietly, standing up. 'It doesn't sound heavy enough.'

Before anyone could reply, the light footsteps suddenly grew faster and heavier. Hudson reacted instinctively and thumped the underside of the roof with his clenched fist.

'Come down and fight!' he cried. 'We're waiting!'

They all swung round as a noise sounded by the window – just in time to see Pugwash, looking very startled, jump down from the roof and run off up the garden.

'Phew! I don't think I can take much more of this,' Ash sighed.

Hudson sat down again and fell very quiet. He stared into space, deep in concentration, his eyes glazing over. It was almost too much for Ash.

Another tense minute passed before Hudson broke the silence again. 'GA is telling me that Mokee Joe is *very* close.'

'How close?' Molly murmured.

And as if in reply, they all heard the distinct clatter of tin cans.

Ash moved quickly back to his place at the shed door and peeped out. He let out a little shriek as he saw the dark shadowy form crouching by the fence, not more than twenty yards away. He slammed the shed door, bolted it and turned towards the others. The beads of sweat on his forehead had grown bigger and were running down his face.

'He's here – Mokee Joe – he's here! I just saw him!'

Hudson could see that Ash was shaking. 'Don't panic!' he said. 'Just sit down and stay as calm as you can. We're going to be OK.'

He tried his best to sound reassuring, but he couldn't blame Ash for being terrified at that particular moment. The atmosphere had been building up all week – right from that very first encounter in the Castle Supermarket. And now it seemed that the dreaded time had finally arrived.

Hudson glanced at his watch.It was 7 o'clock and all was eerily silent again.

Outside, the threatening weather had been slowly closing in and building up.

And suddenly the heavy night air crackled with energy as a bolt of lightning flashed outside. A few seconds later, a long, low rumble of thunder shook Candleshed to its foundations, rattling the door and windows.

Ash screamed.

'I just don't believe this,' Molly said, shaking her head. 'It really *is* like being in a horror film!'

'I want to go home!' Ash wailed.

Molly gave him one of her looks. 'Look, I'm sick of all this waiting around. Why don't we just get out there and have a go at that creep? With my Judo moves, and your new strength, Hudson, I'm sure we can overpower him!'

But then came the sound that sent a shiver down all their spines, even Hudson's – the sound of the door handle slowly turning and creaking as something outside tried to get in.

13

Storms and Spiders

All eyes were focused on the door. Nobody uttered a sound.

The handle continued to turn with a ghostly creaking sound.

'Th-that b-bolt w-won't hold for much longer,' Ash stammered.

'He's right,' Molly whispered. 'It's old and rusted.'

Hudson's eyes never left the door. 'Just stay put,' he said firmly. 'Stay calm.'

The handle stopped turning and everything went deathly quiet again.

And then, without warning, a sharp tapping sound on one of the windows caused them all to jump and swivel round.

They watched with fascination as large raindrops spattered against the pane, each one forming its own little stream and trickling down the glass.

'The storm's coming.'

The three of them watched together as the raindrops got bigger and the tapping against the glass grew louder.

'He's still out there,' Hudson suddenly said. 'I can feel his presence.'

'The storm's getting worse,' Molly said. 'D'you think it might drive him off?'

Ash sounded more cheerful at this suggestion. 'Hey, Hudson – you know she could be right. He doesn't like water, does he? Remember the canal?'

Hudson pressed his nose close to the glass. Outside, it was absolutely black. He couldn't see a thing. 'Nice try, Ash,' he said, 'but this is only rain. It means nothing to him.'

As if to prove Hudson correct, another flash of lightning lit up the window and all three friends jumped back in terror.

There, framed in the blinding light, was the face of Mokee Joe. The lightning struck again and again so that the haggard, grinning countenance lit up with a strobe-light effect, like a Hallowe'en lantern. The evil eyes stared in at them.

They were small, black, bloodshot eyes, full of fury and deeply embedded in the cracked grey flesh. Thin black lips were drawn back tightly over two rows of jagged fangs in a horrible mirthless grin, and the nose looked like layers of scar tissue. Iron studs bordered the face, giving it the appearance of some grotesque warrior's mask. It was the face from Hudson's nightmare

– but this face was real and there was no waking up from it as it sneered through the glass with a most evil glint.

'*Oh God, help!*' Ash screamed, putting his hand over his eyes.

'Hudson, we've got to do something!' Molly cried urgently.

The glass went black again and thunder roared overhead.

Hudson tried to think what to do. Where was Guardian Angel now?

Lightning illuminated the hideous face at the window again, its black eyes penetrating. Hudson could sense that his enemy was thinking – planning its next move.

'Hudson – is he still there?' Ash asked, utter panic in his voice.

'Yes – just stay still.'

'We could use the mobile,' Molly suggested.

'Wait!' It was a command.

Another rumble of thunder caused the windows to rattle. At that moment a large spider crawled down its web from one corner of the pane. It wasn't as big as Spiffy, but it was impressive enough in the flickering candlelight.

The lightning flashed again, illuminating the spider against the face outside. It was now exactly level with Mokee Joe's eyes and the sight of it caused the most amazing reaction from the creature on the other side of the glass.

Hudson watched, awe-struck, as the monster's expression turned from a leer to a look of sheer terror.

'Look, Molly, Ash! He's scared of the spider! Quick, bring the candles over!'

Molly and Ash walked over and held their flickering flames against the window, casting light on the crawling arachnid. They all watched in disbelief as Mokee Joe backed away with a horrible screech, then turned and fled back into the darkness.

Molly and Ash replaced the candles and Hudson began pacing around. 'I just can't believe it,' he kept saying.

'Neither can I,' Ash joined in, sounding slightly more relaxed. 'I mean, who would have bet the creep would be scared of a *spider*?'

Molly sat down. 'Well, Hudson,' she mused, 'they say every enemy has its weakness. I think we've just discovered Mokee Joe's.'

Hudson sat down opposite, put his hands on the back of his head and screwed his mouth to one side. His eyes went to the matchbox marked with a cross, still sitting there undisturbed in the centre of the table. He reached over, picked it up and put it into his trouser pocket.

It was 7.45pm. For a while now, all had been quiet in Candleshed. Hudson and his two friends sat in silence, no-one daring to speak in case they missed a sound that might give some indication of Mokee Joe's next move.

'I'll close the curtains,' Molly said, trying her best to break the tension. 'We can peep through the gaps.'

'Yes, cover the windows and shut out the night,' said Ash. 'I don't want to see that face again!'

But as Molly approached the window facing the garden wall, she suddenly gasped and put her hand to her mouth.

'Hey, you two, come and see this,' she whispered. 'We're back in business!'

Hudson rushed to the window, followed by Ash. They all peered out.

The thunderstorm had moved on and the sky had cleared. The stars twinkled again and a full moon cast its light down into the garden so that the stone wall was lit up in front of them.

At the very top of the wall, two wasted arms were groping their way over, accompanied by the familiar black hat. The three friends watched with panic-filled eyes as the skeletal figure scrambled clumsily down the wall, clinging to old ivy vines or anything else it could grasp with its bony fingers.

Hudson decided to finish the job that Molly had started. He drew the curtains.

'Ash, check that bolt's still secure and keep your mobile on – we may need it.'

Ash did not need telling twice.

'What do we do now?' Molly asked.

'We'll just sit and wait to see what happens,' Hudson whispered.

Silence again. More nerve-racking waiting.

Then, instead of a gentle turning of the handle, there was a very powerful thumping on the door.

'Oh my God!' Ash cried out hysterically. 'He's going to break the door down!'

The thumping got louder and the door threatened to break – the hinges were old and rusted.

'Hudson – we need to do something!' Molly insisted.

Hudson stood up. 'OK – whatever happens next, I want you to follow me out of the door!'

'But Hudson – how—?' Molly cried, her eyes wide. But she did not get time to finish.

With every ounce of strength he could muster and without saying another word, Hudson charged straight at the door. He was amazed how easily it gave way and parted from its hinges. He was even more amazed that there was no sign of the monster outside.

'*Quick – everybody out!*' Hudson yelled.

He grabbed Molly's hand and Ash followed. They used the door as a stepping stone into the garden.

'Where is he?' Molly shouted.

'Yeah, what's happened to him?' Ash asked, looking around in terror.

Hudson pointed back to the door lying on the ground. 'He's under there and probably not too pleased, I reckon!'

That proved to be something of an understatement.

The monster leapt to its feet and squeezed the door between its hands so hard that it cracked and broke into two halves. It threw the remains high into the air and over next door's fence so that they hit the neighbour's concrete yard and splintered.

'OK, let me deal with this!' Hudson shouted. 'Stand back!'

He rushed at the creature again, but this time it saw him coming. As Hudson's right shoulder made contact, it never even flinched, but simply grabbed hold of him and picked him up like a toy, lifting him high into the air and whirling him round by his feet until he felt sick.

'*Let him go! Let him go!*' Molly shrieked.

Hudson wished that Molly hadn't said that because Mokee Joe did as requested. The swirling sensation suddenly stopped and he felt himself being flung a full thirty metres. The only good thing was that he did not land on the concrete. Instead, he had a soft but undignified landing, slap-bang in the centre of the neighbour's compost heap.

Molly backed over towards Hudson, keeping the monster in view. 'Hudson – you OK?'

Hudson tried to speak. His mouth was full of straw and the smell was unbearable. 'I'm fine – take Ash and hide.' He crawled back to the fence and peered over.

But by now Molly had decided it was her turn to face the monster. Her fists were clenched and her face adamant. Meanwhile, Ash moved away up the garden.

'OK!' Molly shouted at the figure in front of her. 'Let's see how you deal with the old judo tackle again.'

Hudson could see that Mokee Joe was staring over her shoulder, his eyes fixed on his real target. It was *him* that the monster wanted, not Molly. In fact, the creature didn't even look at her until it was too late. Once again, Molly dived at his feet, grabbed his legs and brought him crashing to the ground.

'*Yes!*' she whooped. '*He's down!*'

But she didn't have much time to gloat.

'*Molly! Get out of the way!*' Hudson screamed at her. He knew that this time Mokee Joe meant business.

In a fraction of a second the massive creature was back on its feet and Molly was catapulted, with a kicking action, high into the air. She landed with a heavy thud about twenty metres down the garden. Hudson cried out in despair, but then saw to his relief that at least she had landed on soil.

Meanwhile, with his new strength, Hudson had quickly recovered. He leapt back over the fence and faced his enemy again.

But this time it was the fiend that made the first move,

darting towards him with its pincer-like hands ready to grab.

Hudson stood his ground. '*Come on then!*' he yelled, bracing himself. 'Let's see what you're made of!'

The monster grabbed him by the shoulders and tried to push him to the ground. And then the blue glow appeared and electricity crackled through its fingers. Hudson resisted with all his newfound strength, but his body jolted, weakened with the shock.

He's winning – forcing me onto my back, Hudson thought helplessly. *Just like in my worst nightmare.*

And then the creature knelt astride his chest, pinning him firmly to the soil. Looking up into the black, merciless eyes of his attacker, Hudson prayed that he was dreaming again and it was really only Pugwash sitting there. But this was no dream – it was really happening.

Bony hands gripped him around his throat and began to squeeze. A painful, choking sensation closed in on him as the crackling sound grew louder.

I can't breathe, he thought. *GA – if you're there, please help me.*

He started to go dizzy. His time was up – the battle was lost. His eyes went blurred, but he could still see the face of his terminator leaning forward, the taut black lips leering, the harsh studs glistening with oily sweat. He could smell and taste the evil raining down on him.

This is it, Hudson thought miserably. *It's all over.*

14

Just as Hudson thought all was lost, Guardian Angel's words echoed in his head:

'Introduce Mokee Joe to your eight-legged friend.'

The haggard face was pressing ever closer. With his little remaining strength, Hudson just managed to slide the matchbox from his trouser pocket and push the lid open with his thumb. With one final effort he tipped the box and its contents into the brim of Mokee Joe's hat.

'Go to work, Spiffy,' he murmured.

The metal monster simply brushed the box to one side so that it fell onto the ground.

But Spiffy had not been brushed to one side. He'd fallen from the box, anchored himself onto the rim of the hat and was now busy spinning a length of web towards the ground. As the monster prepared to deliver the killer blow, Spiffy made a rapid descent directly in front of its nose.

A shrill scream rang through the cold night air as Hudson felt the bony claws release him.

I'm still alive! Hudson cheered inwardly. He wriggled back and watched as the demonic figure leaped up and ran around in frantic circles, with Spiffy still dangling in front of its nose.

'Molly, Ash – where are you?'

'I'm OK, Hudson. I'm here.' Molly emerged from somewhere down the garden. She looked shaken but still determined. 'Where's that jellyfish Ash?'

'I'm over here!' a voice replied from deep within the runner bean plants. 'Get down here quick. I've got an idea!'

Hudson and Molly crept down to join him while the monster continued its macabre, twisting dance with Spiffy still hanging from its hat.

But when the spider dropped safely to the ground, the demon looked more furious and menacing than ever, casting around to see where its enemy had gone.

'Over here, Dumbo!' Ash yelled from his hiding place.

Hudson and Molly crouched by his side.

'Ash – d'you know what you're doing?' Hudson asked suspiciously.

'It's cool,' Ash replied confidently. 'It's about time I did my bit. Just watch this!'

He stood up and walked out from within his cover so that the monster could see him clearly. 'Come on then – are you scared? Do you want your mummy?'

Molly and Hudson looked at each other in disbelief. Was this really gentle, nervous Ash?

Mokee Joe turned and glowered, then moved slowly, with terrifying deliberation, towards Ash.

Ash took a few steps forward while Hudson and Molly scarcely breathed, waiting to see how his plan could possibly work.

The creature picked up speed. And then, just as it reached the runner beans, Ash stepped cautiously back over the deep trench that only he knew was there. Mokee Joe, who did not know it was there, instantly disappeared from view. For the third time, his world turned horizontal as he crashed headfirst into the rectangular hole that Mr Brown had dug that very afternoon.

'*Ash, brilliant!*' Hudson yelled gleefully. 'And now it's my turn!'

As the monster began to sit up in its ready-made grave, Hudson reached for the spade that his father had left stuck in the soil by the side of the trench. He lifted it with both hands high into the air.

'This is a present from me, Molly and Ash – oh, and from GA as well.' And so saying, he brought the spade down with all his might.

CLANG!

Mokee Joe's hat was hammered flat as the spade rang down on his head. He fell back down into the trench, motionless.

'Hudson – I think you've killed him!' Molly cried out, half in shock and half in triumph.

'No, I don't think so,' Hudson replied. 'He's only stunned. Look!'

The monster was already beginning to stir again and sit up. The three friends watched helplessly as it climbed out of the trench, raised both arms in the air and looked upwards to the night sky.

As it let out a blood-curdling, inhuman howl, they braced themselves for the final attack but to their amazement, the furious creature turned and fled through the neighbour's garden and beyond. They could hear the sound of cracking wood as it flattened fence after fence.

Molly and Ash cried out and hugged each other. 'We've won! He's gone!' they shouted in triumph.

But Hudson still looked serious. 'Not quite,' he said forlornly. 'He'll be back'.

Molly whispered in his ear, 'He's just gone to recharge, hasn't he?'

Molly was no fool.

Hudson looked around at his friends, and at his own filth-smeared limbs. They were all shaken, battered and bruised. 'Yes, he'll be back – and in a much better state than we are!'

He walked down the garden, picked up the matchbox and found his spider friend. Only Spiffy had survived without a scratch.

As Hudson quickly cleaned himself up at the back-door tap, Guardian Angel offered some words of advice.

'To defeat the enemy, keep one step ahead. Don't wait – take the battle to him!'

Hudson understood exactly what Guardian Angel was telling him.

He turned to his two friends, who were also trying to wash off some of the evening's grime.

'Ash, you've done enough. Your plan was brilliant.'

Ash still looked numb but managed to mutter, 'Any time.'

'Could you just do one last thing though?'

'Yes, I suppose so,' Ash said warily.

'Get your mobile and call the police. Tell them we've found the tramp who's been causing all the trouble. Have them meet us at Macalisters in about half an hour.'

'But what . . .? OK – no problem.' Ash walked back towards Candleshed, only too glad to let Hudson get on with it. He knew he'd been brave, but the thought of what he'd done terrified him now more than the act itself.

Hudson disappeared into the brick store at the side of the house and reappeared with his Trekker mountain bike and a torch.

'Hudson,' Molly warned, 'I know where you're going and you're not going on your own!'

'Of course not – get on,' he said with a grim look.

Without hesitating, Molly jumped on the saddle, put her arms around Hudson's waist and clung on tightly. As they sped off down the drive, Hudson couldn't help thinking that she was clinging on a little tighter than she needed to.

15

At 8.15pm, old Mr Stanwick was making his way along Chaucer Road to the Servicemen's Club. He was tootling along on his moped at a top speed of 35 mph when Hudson and Molly hurtled past him on the mountain bike.

The poor man wobbled and skidded to a halt as the two friends sped off, leaving him staring after them in astonishment. He would have some story to tell his grandchildren the next day.

Within five minutes, Hudson and Molly had reached Macalisters and ditched the bike by the perimeter fence. It was now 8.30pm and completely dark.

'Molly, switch the torch off. We don't want him to see us coming.'

Two shadowy forms crawled through the hole in the

fence into the yard of Macalister's Biscuit Factory. Molly switched the torch off just in time; a few seconds later they spotted a security guard with a large dog, obviously out on his rounds.

'Where to now?' Molly whispered.

'The Flour Room,' Hudson whispered back. 'I'll bet my life that's where he is – charging himself up. I just don't understand how a simple thing like flour can be so useful to him.'

A voice in his head reminded him that he and Molly were not alone. '*Flour is almost pure starch,*' the voice said. '*And starch is energy – which is what his body needs. Now hurry – there's no time to waste!*'

They scuttled on like mice and all the time Hudson could sense that Guardian Angel was reading his thoughts.

'Can you see anything?' Molly whispered as they crouched in the entrance to the dimly-lit Flour Room.

'No, but I can hear a moaning sound. Can you?'

They listened intently, their hearts beginning to beat faster.

Molly whispered in a trembling voice, 'Hudson, is it him?'

'Wait – I'll check.' Hudson concentrated his mind. 'No – GA's telling me he's not in here. Pass me the torch.'

Molly handed it over and he switched it on.

One of the flour mountains loomed in the beam. They could see a number of bags ripped open and white powder spilled all over the floor. The moaning was coming from a dark gap in between the stacked pallets. Hudson and Molly aimed the torch; the light picked out a prostrate body dressed in white overalls.

'What hit me?' the man groaned, looking up at the two youngsters.

'I think we know the answer to that,' Hudson replied, glancing at Molly. 'Just stay where you are. We'll get you help as soon as we can – we need to move fast.'

The injured man lay back, clutching his left shoulder.

'Where to now, Hudson? Do you think he's on his way back to Candleshed?'

Hudson thought hard, his eyes closed. The answer came quickly. *'No, he's still here because he knows that you are here,'* Guardian Angel said. *'He's picking up your thought patterns just as I'm picking up his. And I can tell you that there is real evil in his mind. He's fully recharged and determined to strike.'*

And so are we! Hudson thought back. *But where is he?*

'I'm picking up something over to your right, from another building,' said Guardian Angel, *'and I think there may be another one of his victims nearby.'*

Hudson beckoned to Molly, who was crouching by his side.

'Come on. Follow me. I've just picked up some new information.'

They moved out of the Flour Room, across the yard and over towards the Processing Plant.

'Hudson! Look – over there!'

Hudson jumped back as his torch beam illuminated the unconscious form of the security guard.

'But what happened to his dog?' Molly asked grimly.

A soft whimpering answered her question. Hudson shone his torch around and there, over by some oil drums, his beam picked out the stunned animal lying in the shadows. It was cowering back and looked as if it was badly hurt. Hudson guessed it had probably been picked up and thrown in the same way as the poor dog down by the canal.

'Mokee Joe is so evil!' Molly whispered, with real anger in her voice. 'I'm going to . . .'

'We've got to move on,' Hudson urged. 'If Ash has made the phone call, help should be on its way by now.'

But Hudson suddenly stopped dead. Another message was coming through from GA. *'He's in the Processing Plant, hidden behind a huge gold-coloured vat, straight in front of you,'* the voice was saying. *'He's waiting to ambush you.'*

'OK!' Hudson said, gritting his teeth. 'Two can play at his game.'

He relayed the message to Molly, adding, 'We'll double back and go around to the far door so that we can turn the tables on him.'

Molly nodded. 'Great idea. We'll surprise him.'

A few tense minutes later, Hudson and Molly were at the far end of the factory building, peeking tentatively round a metal door. The room hummed eerily to the sound of hissing valves and whirring motors. Belts turned on their conveyors and hot ovens roared with heat. But now there was no-one around. During the night everything was automatic, no ant-like workers busying around as in the day.

Then they saw him.

Skulking there in the shadow of the huge vat, like the vile rodent he was – calculating, waiting, ready to strike. To kill Hudson. A bright bluish-purple glow showed he was fully recharged and prepared for action.

'Look – there he is!' Molly almost yelled, but she controlled herself just in time and barely whispered. 'Do you think he knows we're behind him?'

Hudson continued to glare at the back of his foe with a look of determination. There he was – just as Guardian Angel had said. How he loathed that too-familiar black hat, the greasy hair hanging limply from it, the dirty grey raincoat tied with string. It reminded Hudson of that first encounter, when he'd seen the creature leaning over a frozen food compartment in the Castle. But this time he knew he was a match for it.

Hudson checked with Guardian Angel that they were still undetected. *Does he know we're behind him?*

The answer came through. '*No, because I'm blocking his mind, but I can't keep it up for much longer. You need to act quickly.*'

Hudson looked over his shoulder and saw a length of steel pole lying on the ground. Molly also saw it and needed no telling what to do. *Great minds think alike*, Hudson thought. Without speaking they picked it up and held it in their arms like a battering ram.

Hudson spoke quietly but firmly. 'OK, Molly – you know what to do! We've got to give this everything we've got.'

Molly bit into her top lip and screwed her eyes into little slits. 'Ready when you are.'

As Mokee Joe crouched there, completely unaware of the scene unfolding behind him, they took a deep breath and charged towards his back as swiftly and silently as they could.

'OK, Mokee man!' Hudson said to himself as they picked up pace. 'Now let's see what you're really made of!'

Hudson could feel his new strength surging through the muscles in his arms. Molly thought of the injuries to her friends, the two men and the poor dogs and felt her own muscles tense with hatred for the evil creature.

Hudson fixed his eyes on the end of the pole as it hurtled towards the crouching figure. He was sure that this time they would deliver the killer blow. But just as he and Molly were about to make their mark, the creature heard their footsteps and dived to one side.

'*Watch out – he's dodged us!*' Hudson screamed. But neither of them could stop.

CRUNCH!

The steel weapon struck the gleaming, golden vat. Such was the force of the blow that the pole punctured the tank and hot liquid toffee gushed out onto the ground.

'*What's happening?*' Molly screamed as she felt herself being levered upwards.

'*We missed him!*' Hudson yelled back at her. '*But we didn't miss the vat.*'

Molly was left clinging to the angled pole with her feet swinging off the ground as Mokee Joe rolled over, righted himself and turned to face Hudson. The creature glowed with an intense aura of energy and screeched an unearthly screech.

'Help! Hudson – do something!' Molly begged. 'I'm stuck up here – I can't move!'

Guardian Angel spoke to Hudson. '*You must go straight to the wall and climb the ladder.*'

Hudson looked back towards the metal door and saw a ladder reaching up the wall. He tried to sprint towards it, but very quickly he felt his legs starting to slow down.

'*What's happening?*' he yelled to no-one in particular.

'*Hudson – your feet!*' Molly cried out, still clinging desperately to the pole.

Hudson glanced down and saw that the floor was steeped in a layer of steaming liquid toffee. It was setting and becoming stickier by the second. His shoes were covered in it and he could hardly move his feet.

'Oh God, Molly! This is my nightmare coming true!' he shouted back at her.

Mokee Joe was also having problems, but he was gaining on his target.

'*Untie your laces and kick your shoes off!*' Molly screamed.

Hudson was reluctant to stop moving altogether, but he knew Molly was right. He bent down and started untying his laces.

'Hudson! He's almost on you. Be quick!'

'I'm doing my best!'

As the monster reached out, Hudson finally freed his feet from his shoes, which were now firmly glued to the ground.

'I'm free,' he shouted, 'and the toffee's set! I can run on it!'

'But *he* can't!' Molly whooped in delight. 'Look! He's well and truly stuck.'

Hudson continued running towards the ladder. He glanced back and sure enough, Mokee Joe's feet were embedded in the toffee layer. He began to copy Hudson by untying his laces.

'*Oh no you don't!*' Molly screamed at him.

As Hudson started up the ladder, Molly jumped down from the pole and ran over to their foe. She danced in circles around the enraged monster and did everything she could to distract it from untying its laces. Mokee Joe lashed out at her, the lethal blue sparks shooting from his fingers, but he could never quite reach her as the thick layer of toffee continued to set around his ankles.

'Keep at him, Molly!' Hudson shouted. 'I'll be there in a second!'

Hudson climbed up the ladder waiting for his next instruction. He saw a pipe covered in insulation snaking above his head and he instinctively reached out to it. It felt warm.

'*Climb along this pipe until you are above the monster's head,*' Guardian Angel instructed him. '*You'll need all the strength you've been given.*'

Without question, Hudson did as he was told.

'Hold on, Molly – I'm coming!'

Molly looked up and gasped. 'No – you hold on! If you fall you'll break your neck!'

As Hudson inched his way along, high above Molly's head, he saw that she was still dancing around, tormenting the frenzied creature below. He could also see blue lights flashing in the distance and hear the sound of sirens slicing through the hushed night outside.

OK, Guardian Uncle, Hudson thought, sensing that something special was about to happen and feeling a closer connection with his mentor. *I'm above his head. He's right underneath me. What do I do now?*

Before the answer came, he looked across the factory floor to see an army of police, plain-clothed officials and goodness knows who else come charging through the metal doorway. They all stopped dead in their tracks and looked up at him in disbelief. And then they looked at Mokee Joe. He was almost out of his shoes and about to attack Molly.

'*Hudson,*' the voice in his head said softly, but with a new urgency. '*Focus all your energy on the pipe and pull as hard as you can.*'

'OK, Guardian Uncle – here goes . . .'

Hudson looked up at the thick pipe above his head and began to swing and pull on it for all he was worth. As the pipe began to creak and groan, the crowd below stepped back and gazed upwards. Molly stopped her frenzied dance and she too gazed upwards.

'Molly, get out of the way!' Hudson screamed down at her.

The creature directly underneath looked upwards.

Only Hudson looked down – straight into the face of his enemy.

But this time it was Hudson who was grinning. The creature below was not. Its energetic blue glow had faded and its long fingers had lost their electric spark.

A wrenching, cracking sound echoed through the factory.

'*OK, Mokee Joe!*' Hudson screamed. 'I hope you like hot chocolate!'

The crowd gasped as the pipe finally gave way and Hudson came hurtling down, landing directly on Mokee Joe's head, knocking him into a sitting position with his feet still glued to the ground.

But Hudson did not come down on his own; the contents of the pipe – gallons and gallons of hot, liquid chocolate – accompanied him.

The monster was quickly covered from head to foot in the cascading brown liquid.

The crowd cheered.

'Hudson – you've really done it this time!' Molly shouted, running to help him up.

Together, they looked across at the brown gooey mess that a few minutes earlier had been their most dreaded enemy. The police and officials closed in.

'Molly – this time I think you're right. I think we've won!'

Like the toffee, the chocolate set quickly and it was a strange sight indeed as, five minutes later, a number of police and security officials chipped away with tools of various kinds trying to remove the huge, solid lump that was Mokee Joe from the factory floor. Hudson and Molly watched with the crowd as the encrusted monster was finally carried off and placed in the back of a large van marked 'Government Special Secure Unit' and driven off.

The two friends were led away in triumph, Molly hugging Hudson. He knew that he could never have done it without her. He hoped that Molly would be his friend for life.

They walked to a waiting police car and, a little way off, saw the sergeant and a young policeman helping the injured security guard and his dog into an ambulance. The sergeant looked up and saw Hudson. He stared at him for a moment and then he smiled.

Just then Hudson heard a familiar voice behind him.

'Well, lad, it looks like you've done it again. It seems you're never happy if you're not causing one stir or another.'

But for once, Mr Brown was also smiling. He took off his cap and rubbed his bald head as Mrs Brown ran over and pulled Hudson into her arms.

'Come on, let's have you home and you can tell us everything over some hot chocolate.'

'I think we've seen enough hot chocolate for one night thanks, Mum!'

And they all climbed into Mr Brown's old Morris Minor.

On the journey home, Hudson's Guardian Uncle had a final message for him. '*Well done, son of Hud-3-ergon!*'

Hudson thought for a moment. '*Is that why I'm called Hudson – because I'm the son of Hud?*'

'*Yes, but it's only your Earth identity tag,*' the voice replied.

'*Tell me, why is a creature like Mokee Joe afraid of spiders?*'

'*Ah, many questions again,*' Guardian Angel replied patiently. '*All synthetic Alcatron creatures have a small vent on the side of their necks. If an arachnid or any crawling insect was to get inside, the creature would cease to function in a most painful fashion. Hence, they are programmed to stay well clear.*'

'*Are you still in prison?*' Hudson asked, sensing that time was running out.

'*Yes, but now that they have the real offender, they will soon release me.*'

'*So why can't we meet up again?*' Hudson thought sadly.

'*Before long the Educator will escape and I will need*

to be near to him. We will soon be back in communication. But now I must go. Take care – always remember that on Earth you are very special. And keep your friends close to you – especially the female called Molly.'

'*Please tell me before you go,'* pleaded Hudson, '*the second "E" in "MOKEE" – does that stand for "Educator"?'*

'*Yes, strange though it may seem, the creature is a teacher of sorts.'* The voice was growing fainter now.

'*And Joe? What does that mean?'*

'*The answer to that question may upset you.'* Now the voice was rapidly fading. '*One day it will all become clear . . .'*

And then Hudson's uncle, his Guardian Angel, fell silent.

Why, Hudson wondered, would knowing what Joe meant upset him? What was its significance to him?

But there was no-one now to tell him.

That night, with his enemy under lock and key, Hudson slept deeply in his bed. He dreamt of distant stars and strange planets with red skies and green seas. Children swam and frolicked on beaches of blue sand and none of them had belly buttons.

As Hudson slept, a convoy of vehicles headed for Scotland, towards a special Government Secure Unit situated in a remote part of the Highlands. Amongst the convoy was a specially strengthened van containing the encrusted form of Mokee Joe.

The van bumped and jolted along the winding roads and the driver turned up his heater to take the chill off the cold night air. It never occurred to him that the monster's crusted coating might begin to melt.

Mokee Joe seethed with anger underneath and waited patiently.

ACKNOWLEDGEMENTS

First, I would like to thank Mike Denton and Linda Elvin for all their help, advice, and encouragement, especially in the early stages of the project, and to Vivian Brett for her invaluable help towards the end. Many thanks to them all for their part in making this book look as good as it does.

A big thank you to all the staff, pupils and parents of Cheam School, who have supported me every inch of the way. The pupils of 6CO have proved especially invaluable, acting as my consultants and thus ensuring the authenticity of my young characters.

Finally, a big, heartfelt thank you to Eve White. She has acted as my PA/PR/agent and her amazing energy and enthusiasm have been the driving force that has helped turn a pipe-dream into reality.

Mokee Joe

RECHARGED

Prologue

One fine February afternoon, six members of the Danvers Green Metal Detector Club visited a desolate, marshy area near to the abandoned Norman church of St Michael de Rothchilde. It was believed that a medieval village had existed there and it was hoped that someone might stumble across a few interesting artefacts or even the odd coin or two.

As it turned out, things proved far more interesting.

One of the members decided to sweep a grassy mound on the far side of the church and his detector responded in a very strange way. Further sweeping revealed an unusual expanse of hard metal extending over a large area about four metres below the surface.

Several members dug down to the layer and attempts were made to break off fragments for analysis, but the material proved too hard.

The president of the club notified the authorities and scientists were called in. Using X-rays, it was soon discovered that an impressive elliptical disc lay buried below the marshy ground.

Finally, high-ranking government officials arrived at the scene and subsequently, to the amazement of those present, a strange craft was excavated and hoisted aloft by a huge crane. The object was eventually removed by lorry and taken away for further examination at a Ministry of Defence establishment near the Scottish border.

Members of the metal detector club, local services and the press were legally bound over to keep the bizarre find quiet and undisclosed.

In the months that followed, government scientists examined the craft, holding regular meetings to discuss their findings.

Little did they realise that every move they made was being followed and recorded by a greater mind – a brain so advanced that its power was far beyond their understanding.

Outside the Ministry of Defence Special Unit, just beyond the perimeter fence, a small tent remained hidden between two grassy mounds. Inside, a man with an enlarged head, divided into four distinct lobes, sat cross-legged, staring forward with pupil-less eyes – a faint smile on his craggy face.